PCHS MEDIA CENTER
GRANT, NEBRASKA

D0453770

DATE DUE			

For Pam and Debi

Acknowledgments

My thanks to Mariam Kirby and Monica Spilker

Just Your Type, LLC,

for your assistance with this book.

I want to thank my loyal librarians for buying
my books and supporting me for the long run.

Thanks Tony for your art.
Cover Design by Anthony Conrad

PCHS MEDIA CENTER
GRANT, NEBRASKA

Novels by author:

White Shoulders

Ledges

The Paper Man

Missouri Madness

Shy Ann

Summer of '02

Autumn Letters

This book is a work of fiction and
represents no actual persons living or
dead in any way whatsoever.

August 2005/1st printing/5,000 copies

Copyright 2005
All Rights Reserved

The Vegas Incident

Las Vegas, Nevada.

Summertime, 1985.

Twenty-eight-year-old David Carillo got off work dealing blackjack at the Blue Pond Casino at midnight after a bad night for the house.

"Might get fired," David sniped inwardly, as he removed his flat pack of Pall Mall non-filters from his black vest's side pocket and headed for his parked car. The closer his tall, slim body got to his 1947 Ford sedan, the more he wished he'd had a second double shot of Jack Daniels in his veins. Now he was sure he could see the long red hair of his wife behind the front passenger window.

"Why'd I ever give her that spare key?" he muttered to himself.

He deep-smoked his cigarette as he leaned against the rear fender, thinking how he would wake Gina and tell her he was leaving her for a young Mexican chick who was six months pregnant with his child. That would be it; he knew that his 20-year-old wife was too proud and hot-tempered to ever let him see their son again.

For an instant, as the smoke swirled deep into his lungs, he could see their marriage begin near a canyon wall in Southeast California. The first time they made love together was on Flat Rock, a wide slab of vanilla colored rock that stretched out like a sandstone altar that faced every sunset. It was cold and dark out there on that rock, yet their mating had seemed magical. That was the last time he felt magic in his life.

And there was the image of his son, Ramone. Not even 18 months old, and his parents couldn't get it together.

"Divorce," he whispered in smoke. Thank God my parents aren't alive to see it, he droned inwardly.

He blew out his last drag and stepped on its orange flame with his black patent leather shoe.

Inside his car, he started the engine and purposely turned on the radio to wake her. Gina's green eyes opened and she flicked off Dean Martin.

"Who's with Ramone?" he asked rudely, knowing her Irish blood would boil to life.

"He's with Fran! What do you think...I'd leave him alone in that dive motel you provide for us?"

"Not tonight, Gina. I lost my ass all night. They might fire me."

"Where were you last night?" she demanded.

"Gina...there's no good way to say this. I got this girl pregnant...and I can't stay married to you."

Gina sat there dumbstruck as her husband started to drive out of the casino parking lot. The more she thought about it, the madder she got.

"One of those Mexican whores...right?"

David kept quiet and wary.

"How old is she?"

He made the mistake of smirking when he said she was seventeen. That's when Gina punched him on his ear, causing him to swerve toward a parked car.

"Dammit Gina! Don't hit me while I'm driving!"

"Then pull over so I can knock your teeth out!"

Again she punched at his head, but he dodged it and quickly pulled over to the side of the road.

2

"I want a divorce, Gina! I can't live like this with two babies!"

"You mean three babies! Seventeen for God's sake!"

"She's only a year younger than you were," he said.

"Yes...and we got married! You're nearly thirty, David! When are you going to grow up?"

"I'm not driving with you in this car. You'll have to walk from here," he said, rubbing his sore ear. The engine idled in neutral.

"I'm not getting out of this car. You'll have to drag me out."

Things got crazy with fists flying and feet kicking. It took all of David's strength to force Gina out the front passenger door and onto the pavement. He couldn't close the door and lock it fast enough; they were fighting again on the front seat. This time Gina managed to get on the driver's side of the front seat with her penny loafers kicking hard.

David yanked her out of the car and flung her far enough away so he could lock all his doors. But before he could drive away she sprawled on his engine hood with her hands gripping the windshield wipers.

"Get the hell off, Gina!"

David started to drive, slowly, then braking to see if she'd slide off the maroon hood. No luck. Then he steered side-to-side with more and more speed, until finally she flew off the hood on his side of the car. In his side-view mirror, he saw Gina's lower body run over by a laundry truck, a squat-boxed green truck that had once been a Jewel-T truck.

Instead of stopping, David took off. In his mirror he could see that the truck stopped and the driver got out to help Gina.

In a haze of desperation, David Carillo drove to the

Shamrock Motel. Fran, Gina's neighbor and friend, was awakened by David's loud knock.

"Who is it?" she queried from behind her locked door.

"David...Ramone's father."

She cracked the door and peered out at the disheveled blackjack dealer.

"Gina's at the apartment...passed out. I came to get Ramone so he's there when she gets up. She wants us all to go to breakfast together."

Within two hours David was headed south for California with his son asleep on the back seat surrounded by hastily stacked piles of the boy's clothes and jars of baby food.

Blake

Blake had been constructed in the late 1930s to house Mexican migrant farm workers who toiled sixteen hour days in California's Imperial Valley. The one-story stucco structure was named Blake after the man who built it; eight Mexican families once lived there.

It looked like an abandoned motel from Interstate 8, standing on the north side of the highway at the last exit before the climb, or the first exit after the descent from the Vallecito Mountains toward San Diego a hundred miles to the west.

Blake sat 26 miles west of El Centro, and right on the eastern border of the Cuyapaipe Indian Reservation, where the Carillo family had been raised.

Now, six hours after fleeing Vegas, David waited in his car outside Blake, feeding Ramone his breakfast.

He waited until he saw his younger brother Richard come out one of the eight doors. Twenty-two-year-old Richard Carillo lived there with his new wife, Lola, and their 3-month-old baby girl, Maria. They were the only residents in Blake. Richard had rented the building for only two hundred bucks a month from Robert, their middle brother. Robert Carillo was the prosperous brother of the trio.

David got out of his car holding Ramone in his

arms. Astonished to see his brother, Richard called his wife outside. She was a full-blood Latino from Mexico. The Carillo brothers were full-blood Cuyapaipe, an agrarian Native American people who had lived on this land for thousands of years.

David handed the baby to Lola, who took the little boy inside so the brothers could talk.

"I'm in big trouble, Richard."

David lit a cigarette as his quiet, patient brother waited for an explanation.

"I was involved in an accident in Vegas. Gina and I had a fight. She wouldn't get out of my car. Things got bad when I locked her out. She got onto the hood and I got crazy and hit the gas. She fell off and was run over by a truck."

"Is she dead?" Richard's stolid face was unreadable.

"Maybe, I don't know. I didn't stick around. I got Ramone and came here to see if you and Lola would keep him. I couldn't stay in Vegas, or leave Ramone there."

"That's big trouble for you, brother."

"I know. See...I got this Mexican chick pregnant and I wanted a divorce from Gina. I gotta go south till this blows over. I can't go to jail."

"You will if you run...for sure. You should go back to Vegas and turn yourself in."

"I can't. I've been stealin' from my table, a couple grand a month. My boss'll kill me. I was gonna pay it back with a good run, but I kept losin' my ass."

David handed his brother Ramone's clothes and left-over food. "Thanks, Richie, for taking my son. I'll owe you."

"Yeah, you will."

"They'll know I was here when they find Ramone here. Tell them you found the boy at your door."

Richard stood facing the morning sunlight, squinting through the dust left behind by his brother's car heading for I-8. His oldest brother was a lot of things, but not a liar. He had stolen money and abused his wife. Prison would destroy a man so unregimented, for David had to be free, never confined. That was his nature, that was his place.

When Lola saw her husband in the doorway with his arms full of baby clothes, she saw that his sad eyes carried bad news.

Dead South /New Life

Gina was lucky to be alive, but she never felt that way. For ninety days she languished in intensive care, unable to think of anything but her baby, Ramone. The word 'paraplegia,' paralyzed from the waist down, didn't bother her nearly as much as her son being kidnapped by the man who, the police said, probably fled to Mexico after leaving the child on the Carillo doorstep.

Two days ago, she had been able to talk to Richard and Lola on the phone and was relieved to know Ramone was in good hands. Gina had met Richard before she married David and knew he was a good man. Lola assured Gina that she could care for two babies until she recovered.

"You'll never walk again," her doctors pronounced. But that would never stop the fiery redhead from raising her son; she believed that with all her heart and soul.

Yet, when she was helped into a wheelchair for her first ride around the hospital halls, instead of freedom, she felt only helplessness as an orderly pushed her chair past dozens of open doors.

On Gina's third day out of bed, she received a message from one of the nurses stationed on the maternity ward. One of the new mothers was giving her baby to the state. The girl had said the father of her baby was David Carillo, Gina's husband. The girl knew that Gina was in the same hospital and thought she ought to know about the baby.

Gina asked to be wheeled to the mother's room so she could talk to her about the whereabouts of her lousy husband. The nurse informed Gina that the Mexican mother had walked out of the hospital.

Behind the maternity ward glass, baby Victor Carillo was held by the nurse and shown to the wheelchair-bound patient, who wept at the awful way baby Victor was starting his life.

Gina went to see Victor every day during viewing hours. The boy's black hair and black eyes were a perfect match to David's. Victor looked more like David's son than Ramone, who had inherited light skin and green eyes from his mother.

When she was allowed to hold Victor, her heart embraced the baby boy, she began to plan. She convinced Richard and Lola to bring Ramone to her for a visit. Then she introduced Richard to his nephew. With only days remaining before Victor was due to be put up for adoption, Lola and Richard fell in love with David's tiny son.

Gina's relentless petitioning for Victor to be placed in the Carillo home was successful. The same day Richard and Lola took custody of the boy, Gina was released from the hospital. She rode back to El Centro to live with her son and extended family in Blake.

Seated in the back of Richard's ramshackle Buick with little Ramone and Maria, Gina watched Lola cooing to Victor. She was thrilled to be reunited with her own son, and content for the first time in years, knowing that they would have a real home at last.

She could hear the metallic rattle of her wheelchair in the trunk behind her. She was moving on.

Life at Blake

Gina's disability and aid to her dependent child drew $300 a month, which she gave to Richard. Richard was the manager of El Centro's only movie theater, The Jupiter. Most mornings, Richard was able to work on the remodeling of Blake for his doubled family of six.

He soon put three of the bathrooms in working order; and he knocked out one bedroom wall so Gina's north-facing bedroom was not so cramped and she could wheel herself in and out with ease.

Gina's black and white TV was conveniently positioned on a shelf two feet from the floor. Within eight months Richard had finished Ramone's room next to his mother's room, and joined together two kitchens with separate dining areas, to Lola's relief.

Though Ramone and Maria were three years away from starting school, Gina became their preschool teacher, instructing them from her chair. Even Lola sat in with baby Victor while Gina read from stacks of books delivered by the Imperial County Bookmobile.

Lola was also learning English with the children, improving greatly day by day. The teacher was serious about the Carillo household speaking English as the dominant language, imploring Lola to speak her native language as little as possible. Gina often told Lola that one day all of the children would be in college, a dream Lola and

Richard wanted for their children more than anything.

Medication bottles were always stacked on Gina's bedside table, and frequently abused during bouts of gin drinking on weekends, when she harangued the younger woman.

"I can't stand so much grease in your meat, Lola! For God's sake, Lola, learn to cook lean for all of us!"

A year passed with few changes. Gina remained bitter. Monthly tirades would erupt over David and how the law wasn't looking for him in Mexico.

"Two years! And nothing! You can't tell me there is justice in this world!" Gina railed.

Ramone was getting old enough to be confused by his mother's sobbing, most every night, coming through his bedroom wall. He would awake to her plaintive sobs, rising above the sound of her TV set. Lola was aware of Ramone's plight, often telling her husband that his room should be moved closer to Maria and Victor. Richard knew better, telling his wife in his quiet way, "Gina wants her only child close to her, just as we want out children close to us."

Nine Palms

The summer before Ramone was to start school, the Carillo family were headed for Nine Palms for a family picnic with Robert and Monica Carillo. Robert was the successful middle brother of the three Carillo boys raised on reservation land at Ocho Canyon, located six miles northwest of Blake.

Robert had torn down the Carillo family adobe house where the three brothers grew up and he built a fabulous, one-story, adobe ranch-style home with running water and a generator that powered electricity which gave them hot water. Since Robert was the first son to marry, he was allowed to live at Ocho Canyon when their mother died.

Robert became a well known natural healer of his tribe through his wife's penchant for herbal gardening. Robert and Monica were responsible for perfecting a toxin-cleaning remedy that killed deleterious intestinal parasites and enabled the body's organs to heal naturally from many diet-related ailments.

Robert collected juices from a rare cactus that grew exclusively on their 360 acre canyon property. Since Monica had been raised on the same reservation land as her husband, they were both aware of the miracle cures told in family legends surrounding the rare blue cactus.

The formula that Robert and Monica created and

which, by law, could only be grown and sold on the reservation, drew customers' vehicles from all over the southwest. Robert named his formula Purple 8, because of its purple color when oxygenated. The 8 came from the figure-8 shape of the older blue cactus orbs, spiny arms wrapped in figure-8s and never seen outside of Ocho Canyon, land named by past generations of Natives who had learned Spanish long before English.

Robert's station wagon arrived at Nine Palms a half mile northwest of Blake on reservation ground. Nine palm trees standing thirty feet tall in a circle cast a patch of shade as big as a house. The graveled road beside it was littered with debris dropped by trespassers. Richard's Buick was parked there.

Richard had told Lola and Gina that Nine Palms was a place where Robert brought Latinos from Mexico to give them 'sessions' involving his Purple 8 formula.

The children ran about the shady oasis as the adults emptied the vehicles of their picnic food and colorful handmade blankets. Richard and Robert together wheeled Gina over the rough ground and positioned her in the shade so she could watch the children playing.

Robert was stout like a bull and healthy in appearance, more so than the other brothers. Monica was short and attractive with raven-black hair that reached her waist in one braid.

Gina had met them several times, usually at Blake or Ocho Canyon during holidays. Discord between them was Gina's doing. She made light of their healing abilities, cynically calling each of them "Doc." The fact that the couple had recently legally changed their last name to "Ocho" only gave Gina more fuel for her bitter nature. That was Gina's place.

Now, as the other adults carried over things for the picnic, Gina watched the children pointing at the purple stains on the shaded earth. As Lola and Monica spread blankets on the ground, Gina quipped, "No purple blankets?"

Robert loved being with the children. He and his wife could not conceive a child and were considering adopting, after seeing how happy Richard and Lola were to have Victor.

Uncle Robert hoisted each child high in the air, kissing and hugging, enthralled with the children's laughter. Robert's keen eyes noted that Ramone was too sullen for a young boy. That was Gina's influence, he knew. Just as he knew that the gin bottle inside the leather pouch strapped beside her lifeless left leg was numbing her pain. He was positive he could help Gina with his formula, but she refused to try it.

"Ramone! Where's my lighter?" Gina barked.

Ramone stopped running around the palms with Maria and Victor. Monica and Robert watched Ramone walk purposely toward his mother's chair, then dig his little hands deep into her pouch where he fished out her favorite refillable yellow lighter, purchased in another life in a Las Vegas souvenir shop. Then, with a long Tarryton clamped between his mother's lips, the boy flicked the lighter and raised the flame to her craned head and lit her cigarette.

"Thank you, sweetie."

Ramone rejoined the kids, circling round one of the nine palms, yet Robert could see the boy peeking at his mother, as if something was on his mind.

The night before, Ramone had listened to his mother's telephone conversation as he lay in bed thinking about today's picnic. She had been complaining to her sister in Los Angeles, going over all the details about how "David left me in the street to die like a dog."

It was the guttural enmity in her voice that scared Ramone into a sweaty ball of confusion. How could my father do that? he wondered.

It was a nice picnic, though, with civil conversation for the most part, until Monica suggested to Gina that she come to a Purple 8 session at Ocho Canyon. A few shots of straight gin fueled her curt reply, "Are you a doctor?" After her question was greeted by an awkward silence she continued, "When you finish medical school, let me know!" She laughed haughtily.

The Jupiter

The Jupiter Theater was located in downtown El Centro. Most of downtown was on Central Avenue, a wide street offering a variety of services for traffic that had gotten off I-8 searching for gas and food.

The single-screen theater was an important source of family entertainment for locals, so Richard kept it very clean and brought in new releases that were appropriate for family viewing. Any R-rated films were shown after 9 PM on weekdays and weekends. PG movies were shown earlier in the evenings, and weekend G-rated matinees were reserved for the youth of Imperial County.

Over the past few years the Carillo children had discovered all of The Jupiter's secret places. They played hide and seek behind the heavy curtains and in dark nooks, on weekends, when Lola cleaned the restrooms and helped her husband with the bookkeeping.

Maria would follow the boys into the dark projection room, where Victor, alert beyond his years, explained every step needed to show a movie. Richard had taught his son everything he knew, splicing film together when it snapped apart during a viewing.

That was boring stuff for Ramone; he was more interested in finding the hidden places backstage where nobody ever went. Maria stood in the shadows watching with awe as her cousin climbed up to the top of the velvet curtain via a series of pegs on the wall, whereupon he would pretend to fall, only to grab one of the two emergency ropes, ready to open the curtains in case the electrical runner shorted out, or there was a power failure. Ramone had powerful legs inherited from his mother's people, legs that scissor-straddled the rope with such force that it seemed to Maria that he didn't need to use his arms, his legs would hold him with ease, if he wanted.

In total darkness during show time, the trio would duck-walk behind the screen, staying below the white portion so their shadows could not be seen. The rumbling music, or dialog blaring from the theater speakers high above them made their bodies vibrate, and they smothered their laughter behind their hands. At times the film's musical score would scare them back to their seats in the rear of the auditorium near the aisle running lights, where Richard could see them from the projection room.

At the end of the show, Ramone got a whisk broom and dustpan from the utility closet, then he'd grab a steel brush and wet some rags to use on the gum and candy stuck to the floor. Little Victor took garbage bags for himself and Maria, then when everyone was out of the theater and the lights were on, Maria would start at the front row and Victor at the back, picking up any trash. Richard paid them each a dollar.

At times, the kids found possessions left behind, or dropped by patrons: sweaters and coats, purses and billfolds, coins and paper money. Richard told them that they could split any money found, unless a customer came back for it. Over time the lost and found grew until Richard called the Salvation Army to pick up the items.

By the autumn of 1992, despite the fact that his family enjoyed his workplace, Richard knew that his salary of eighteen thousand dollars a year would never be enough to allow him to save for the children's college. Richard had applied for an upcoming management position at Jupiter North, in Omaha, Nebraska, that paid an annual salary of twenty-six thousand dollars, and included complete medical coverage for his household. The position would open the first of the year. The best part was that the departing theater manager lived in a large two-story brick house just three blocks from the theater, and was willing to rent the house to the incoming manager for only $350 a month for a three-year period.

Lola and Richard discussed it every night at bedtime, going over all the possible negatives involved in such a big move. Thanks to Gina's home tutoring, all the children were doing well in grade school. Ramone was now breezing through the 3rd grade. His cousins were both in the 2nd grade, after the school skipped Victor forward from kindergarten.

Gina was the biggest question mark. If she wouldn't move her son north, Richard refused to go without them. Unity was a genetic thing that flowed in the Carillo blood. Even David had it. That's why he left Ramone with family instead of abandoning the boy in Las Vegas.

Lola agreed with her husband: if Gina stayed—the family stayed at Blake.

Now they waited for Gina's decision. They had talked to her several times, answering as many of her questions as they could. One Sunday, while the entire family viewed the matinee at The Jupiter, Gina's chair was parked in the handicap aisle with Lola and Richard seated in front of her. Minutes before the show was to start, while the kids were still at the concession stand, Gina leaned forward and whispered, "I've decided we'll go north with you. I can't have Ramone caring for me alone."

"We wouldn't go if you didn't want to," Lola whispered and extended her hand to Gina.

"I know, dear. We're a family...and families are supposed to stay together," Gina replied.

Richard nodded in agreement, then turned back to Gina. "What about taking Ramone away from school here?"

"That was my only concern. I won't tell him until he's on Christmas break, so it's not on his mind in school. I think it's best not to tell Maria and Victor, either, until I tell Ramone." Lola and Richard nodded in agreement.

As the son of the eldest Carillo brother, Ramone's right to inherit Ocho Canyon when he married was in her decision to move away. Gina decided she would tell her son of his legacy when he graduated from high school and was headed for college. She did not want her son marrying young as she had. Besides that, she did not want to separate Ramone from Victor; not only was he Ramone's best friend, she knew that brilliant Victor would help Ramone succeed in school, and that would help him get the financial aid he would need, since she didn't expect a single dime of support from David.

"Ramone will like a bigger city when he's older," Gina whispered to Lola's agreeing nod.

"That means he'll have to jump right into a new school with new kids after Christmas break," Richard said softly.

"I know. He'll be fine."

Richard warned Gina, "It will be real cold in January, a big climate change."

"Richard," Gina said, laughing, "Ramone and I have Irish blood in our veins. We're natural survivors. It's you, Lola, Victor and Maria who will have the hardest time adjusting."

19

Christmas Break

In early December, Richard left for Omaha in a used GMC panel truck, pulling a large closed trailer that held their living room furniture and half of their belongings. He felt good knowing he could get the rest of their stuff when he returned to pick up his family.

Robert had promised to stop by Blake once a week to take Lola grocery shopping. He told his younger brother not to worry, that when he returned on Christmas Eve the whole family would spend Christmas at Ocho Canyon before they left for Omaha.

The kids always picked up the school bus in front of Blake with Gina's and Lola's eyes on them as they boarded, and again as they returned home.

On the 20th of December, the last day of school before Christmas break, Gina asked Lola to wheel her out to the Blake bus stop to meet the kids.

With her kelly green winter coat and striking red hair, his mother looked like Christmas to Ramone as he leaped from the yellow bus, beaming, holding up his report card with its five bright red stars.

On the way home, Lola pushed the wheelchair slowly while Gina raved on and on about every subject and all those beautiful stars that mesmerized Maria and amused Victor. Then, Gina broke the news to all the children.

"Guess what, kids? I have exciting news! Right after

Christmas we are moving to a big city up north!"

"Is that why Daddy took our stuff?" Maria asked.

"Yes!" Lola said.

"I knew he wasn't selling our stuff like you said he was," Ramone informed his mother.

"Me, too," Victor said.

"We didn't want to worry you about a big move. It's a Christmas surprise we have been saving for now." Gina smiled. "We'll be in a big new house and you will go to new schools."

"Better than here?" Maria asked.

"Yes!" Lola promised.

Gina examined all the report cards with Lola looking over her shoulder. "I'm proud of all of you! We'll take these to your new school and show them what you did here!" Gina hugged and kissed her pupils in turn. "How does that sound?" she asked.

"Good!" the children exclaimed joyfully.

"The best part is that we're all staying together!" Gina added.

"Victor, get the door for us please." Lola smiled at the boy. Gina looked up at Lola's smiling eyes as if all went well.

On Christmas Eve, Richard returned home with the empty trailer and celebrated his return with his family. At dinnertime he sat at the head of the table with Gina parked at the other end. Even the women were as awestruck as the children while they listened to Richard's description of their new home and watched as he drew its likeness with crayons on a white sheet of paper.

"It's brown brick and shaped like this. It is a solid house with four bedrooms. This is Gina's room and this is Lola and Richard's bedroom," he laughed.

PCHS MEDIA CENTER
GRANT, NEBRASKA

"Where's my room?" Maria exclaimed with her bright brown eyes glowing.

He printed Maria's name in an empty square to her delight. "And this will be Ramone and Victor's room." He printed two names in a larger square for the gape-jawed boys.

After drawing the front and back door and the front and back yard, he drew the large living room and kitchen.

"How many bathrooms?" Gina asked.

"Three. One on the main floor and two upstairs."

"I hope my room is on the first floor," Gina laughed after adding, "unless you want to carry me downstairs every day."

"Yes! Of course your room is on the main floor," he laughed while sketching the basement and told everyone how it would become a play area for the kids. The new house even had a laundry room where they could wash their clothes.

Lola smiled at her husband and said, "You mean where I can wash the clothes.

Legend of Flat Rock

After Christmas Eve dinner, Robert came over to help his brother load the rest of their belongings into the trailer. The trailer was jammed to its roof and held everything except travel clothes, ensuring that the family would not be crowded in the panel truck.

Later that night, Robert drove the family to Ocho Canyon to spend Christmas there. The drive to this secluded Native land that the Carillo family had occupied for hundreds of years was a circuitous, gradual climb on a desert canyon, one-lane, dirt road that few locals ever traveled. The road was too rocky and bumpy for any activity except keeping their heads from banging into the car windows.

Arriving at the home's rock-lined driveway that curved and straightened for 200 yards, the car continued until the road ended in front of the salmon colored adobe home perched on the rim of Ocho Canyon.

Entering the house, the foyer had a low ceiling, yet after a few steps the ceiling vaulted to twenty feet with three skylights to catch the sun. The tile floors had been made in Mexico by one of Robert's Purple 8 clients. The main room was large; glass covered the west side of the room. During daylight, the windows revealed the ever changing light of Ocho Canyon, which began at the edge of a tiled back patio shaded by three young palms.

Rich Mexican wood shone its dark luster in the solid furniture upholstered in brown leather. Picture frames around Native American original oil paintings hung throughout the main room among colorful textiles woven by native hands. Large Navaho rugs splayed out on the floors of all the rooms of this fabulous family home known as Casa de Ocho Canyon.

Maria and Victor went straight for the 12-foot Christmas tree; they were enthralled by the most beautiful decorations they had ever seen. That was Monica's gift to her departing family, along with the perfectly wrapped presents in bright red, green, and gold paper and colorful ribbons arranged under the tree, each with a tag bearing the lucky name designated for such a carefully prepared gift.

Ramone wandered over to the tree, but didn't camp there as the other kids; he preferred to observe everything from a distance. He knew he was leaving this part of his world and going away for a long time; he was moved to save the moment for some inexplicable reason.

Right after opening presents early Christmas morning, the children followed Richard and Uncle Robert out the patio door and headed for the heart of Ocho Canyon. Down they went on a narrow path surrounded by sagebrush and dry, cracked earth. Robert led the way with Richard trailing the children. Both men carried large canteens filled with water strapped over their shoulders.

The kids were even more thrilled now than they were when they attacked their presents. Last night, Uncle Robert had told them a bedtime story about the Legend of Flat Rock in Ocho Canyon. Robert had a way of telling a story like nobody else. All three children lay together with spooked eyes on the queen-size bed in the guest bedroom.

Robert began, "Many years ago, a young man of our

people discovered a blue cactus deep into Ocho Canyon. This blue cactus had arms shaped like the number 8. The young man was very thirsty, so he took his knife and cut into the blue cactus to get a drink. The juice was purple and tasted sweet, so he drank more of this purple juice rather than die of thirst. On his way back through the canyon, he became dizzy. Then he came upon a huge flat rock that was shaded by the canyon wall. He decided to rest there until the sun went down. He fell into a deep sleep. When he awoke it was late at night. He was terribly scared because he discovered a giant snake, glowing purple, stretched out beside him on the flat rock. He could not move. He was too frightened. When he looked at his arms he was really scared because they were the same color of purple and glowing just like the giant snake. Soon the snake curled itself into a figure 8 around the terrified man. The man trembled, trapped inside one of the two loops made be the snake's long purple body. He couldn't move for fear that the snake would bite him. So, under a full moon, he sat there all night, until he fell asleep slumped over like this." Uncle Robert demonstrated to the wide-eye children.

"What happened, Uncle Robert?" Victor asked.

"In the morning the man awoke to see that his arms were back to their normal color and the purple snake was gone. But he looked down and could see that the rock surface around him was stained purple...like it is to this very day. Native people sought out the place they named Flat Rock, where a person could pray for one wish to come true, while sitting inside the loops of the purple 8 stain."

"Did their wishes come true?" Maria asked her uncle.

"Yes! But only if they told their wishes to the friends who gathered there as witnesses. So now I want each of you to think of the one wish you would like to come true. I will take you into the canyon tomorrow so you can make your wish inside the purple 8 on Flat Rock. But do not speak of your wish tonight."

For hours the children lay in bed quietly thinking of their wishes, forgetting all about Christmas morning. Even while opening presents with the family, the three kept asking their Uncle Robert when they were going to Flat Rock.

Now, as Robert led them up the slippery incline toward the legendary rock, he too was anxious to hear their wishes. When all five of them stood on the vanilla colored surface of Flat Rock, the men smiled to see the kids staring down in awe at the large purple 8 stain.

Robert asked Richard to sit inside one of the figure 8 loops, while he sat inside the other loop. The two men faced each other, crossed their arms, and clasped hands, making another figure-8.

Robert explained, "We each close our eyes and make one special wish that we want to come true. When we can see that wish coming true in our imagination, we open our eyes and tell the other person what the wish is."

The children stood wide-eyed in wondrous captivation watching the men.

"Open your eyes, brother Richard, when you are ready to reveal your wish."

Richard basked in the palpable joy the children emanated around him. When he opened his eyes he could see their little faces on him as he said, "I wish that our long trip to our new home is a safe one."

"Very good!" Robert clapped his hands and that made the children applaud with him. Then Robert revealed his wish.

"My wish is that you are all happy and healthy in your new home."

Richard applauded with the children.

"Now, Victor, take your father's place," Robert said.

Little Victor, with shining black eyes, sat in the loop and held crossed hands with his uncle.

"Close your eyes and see your wish, Victor. When you see your wish, open your eyes and tell us what it is."

It was obvious Victor was trying hard to see his wish. Finally the dark-skinned boy opened his eyes and proclaimed, "I wish that I can become a famous artist."

"Very good!" Robert led the applause.

Now Maria took her brother's place, her white teeth showing joy as she crossed hands with her uncle and closed her eyes. Her face took on a dreamy expression.

"Do you see your wish, Maria?"

The little girl nodded with such a smile that it made Richard's heart flutter. She opened her brown eyes and said, "My wish is to always be happy every day."

"That's a beautiful wish, Maria." Robert smiled as Richard picked up his little girl and kissed her cheek.

Ramone's turn. Robert could see that his nephew was very serious about his wish as he entered the 8; the boy pressed his lips together and waited with eyes closed until tears began to drip from beneath his eyelids.

"Do you see your wish, Ramone?" Robert asked gently as he held his nephew's sweating hands. Ramone shook his head no.

"Keep your eyes closed...and see your wish. No hurry. See it coming true. Take your time...and see it coming true."

"I can't!" Ramone cried.

"That's okay. I want you to imagine a purple 8 floating above your favorite place in all the world. It's a perfect number 8 that is purple. You do have a wish, right?" The boy nodded yes, sniffing from his tears, as Robert continued softly, "Now see your wish coming true in your special place as you draw your purple 8 there." They waited until a smile came over Ramone's pale face. Robert asked him if he could now see his wish. He nodded yes with a smile. "Now keep seeing it more and more. Then take it out of your special place, open your eyes, and tell us your wish."

Four anxious faces were on him when Ramone opened his eyes and said, "I wish my mother could walk."

Everyone applauded loudly and tears came from the men.

Jupiter North

It was 1996. Ramone was 12, Maria 11 and Victor 10. All the kids were doing well in the Omaha elementary school where Lola worked part-time in the school's cafeteria. Richard was happy managing Jupiter North; his salary had been raised to thirty-six thousand dollars a year. He was certain he had made the right move in coming to Omaha. They were comfortable in their sprawling house, located just west of downtown in a clean middle class ethnic neighborhood peopled by men and women who had worked long hours to get ahead.

Gina remained home alone when Lola worked during the school year. Ten hours a week she did water therapy at the YMCA pool not far from the house. Gina's exercise regimen kept her attitude more positive even though there was no movement from her lower body.

Two years earlier, David had been busted in Tucson for transporting marijuana from Mexico. His five-year sentence suited Gina, since he had never been charged with leaving the scene of her "accident." David had written to his estranged wife from his Arizona prison cell last Christmas, telling her how sorry he was about what happened in Las Vegas. When he was released, he promised, he would make it up to her. When Gina received the letter, she had an attorney serve him with divorce papers. David's plea for forgiveness had been answered by a curt note that had two

29

words: "Drop dead." The divorce had been finalized just two months ago.

Maria had become the happy girl she wished to be. Victor was the best artist in his class. Ramone was still sullen and kept to himself, without friends either in school or in the neighborhood. Maria and Victor were his only companions. Ramone, as the oldest, was far more serious than his cousin and half-brother. That was his place. He watched more TV than the other kids in the Carillo house, spending hours at a time in his mother's room watching shows with her. Gina loved dramas and the company of her son.

Every Saturday, Richard took the kids to work with him. The matinee was great fun for Victor and his sister. Ramone preferred to roam around the theater that was much larger than The Jupiter in El Centro. Ramone found many secret places where he could hide from view behind the curtain or up in the balcony that was kept closed during matinees. He could always watch a movie at home, but here inside the massive Jupiter he could get away from the constant demands of his mother.

Since the weather changed often in Omaha, Gina's aches and pains increased and bounced around like the Omaha barometer. Her medication bottles had grown in number, stacked in rows on her bedside table. And she was aging fast: her light skin was wrinkling, and she was losing her hair. What hair remained was thinning to red strands that flew about whenever she moved in her chair. Worst of all, she was consuming more gin day and night, and chainsmoking.

Jupiter North became Ramone's place of escape. Here he could be alone, away from his mother's harping and mood swings that made his life miserable. He wished he could be like Victor and Maria, carefree, without worry about the future. They were the beautiful and lucky ones with dark skin and wavy hair, combined with perfect white teeth.

Ramone came to the dark theater to hide from his own ugliness, an ugliness he believed he inherited from his mother since "the accident." Why was it so easy for Maria and Victor to sit there and be lost in every movie every Saturday? he scoffed inwardly.

Then, to get away from his busy mind, he would find a secluded seat in the shadows of the closed balcony and imagine his purple 8 as he had at Ocho Canyon. He had saved every letter his uncle had written him. Robert's words gave him hope. They were words like the ones his uncle spoke on Flat Rock when he couldn't see his wish. Now when he closed his eyes to see his purple 8, he could make it swirl in never-ending loops, because Robert had told him to see only his purple 8, with no mind activity, no other thoughts. "And the longer you do this, Ramone, the more you will attract positive circumstances in your life. Your life will change for the better. Learn to quiet your mind so that you can live in the present. Then, if your mother never walks again, you will at least handle that reality and be free of her pain."

There he would sit, in the dark balcony of Jupiter North, his senses oblivious to the movie, and focus on his purple 8. Five minutes...then ten...the longer the better, he told himself. He would catch his mind drifting into other thoughts, yet he stayed in his seat tracing his purple 8, trusting that his uncle's words were the key to making his life better. He told no one that he had overheard his mother say to Lola that he was the eldest Carillo son of his generation and would inherit Ocho Canyon, home of his ancestors for hundreds of years.

When the movie was over and the house lights came on, he was not the same ugly boy with a mind full of ugly, negative thoughts, spinning into the same downward spiral as his mother. When Richard drove them home, as Victor and Maria chattered away about the movie, Ramone focused on his purple 8, truly listening to the conversation around him. For once he was not thinking of things to say, or judging their idle chatter.

Ramone smiled at the gift his Uncle Robert had given him on Flat Rock, and in the letters hidden in his dresser drawer. Tonight he would write his uncle and tell him he was able to see his purple 8 for a long time, and that he was feeling better about things.

Purple Crap

In 1998, David was paroled from prison. He enclosed several letters to Ramone in letters to his brother Robert, which Robert forwarded to Ramone. David told Ramone in every letter how sorry he was about his mother's condition. His told his son everything that had happened in Las Vegas.

"Things got so crazy that night, Ramone. I take full responsibility for driving my car when she was on the hood. Ninety-nine times out of a hundred, that accident would never have happened. But it did. I am truly sorry for the pain I have caused your mother and you. You will never know how much I regret that terrible night."

In a letter, Robert told Ramone that his father was taking Purple 8 on Flat Rock, three sessions so far in two months. He reported how well his brother was responding to the treatments that involved drinking the purple juice from the blue cactus, which killed intestinal parasites, and brought out toxic emotions that his father had accumulated during his life before and in prison.

In closing, Robert had said that both he and David wished that Gina would try a Purple 8 session. Robert would be willing to fly to Omaha, if she ever agreed.

That was the beginning of ugly chaos between Ramone and his mother. Ramone made the mistake of showing her the letters from Robert and David.

"You can just go live with that bastard!" Gina swore at her son from her wheelchair.

"But Mom! I know it can help you with your pain! I only want to help you!" he pleaded after she threw the letters at him.

"If you want to help me, you can get your worthless father to send me fourteen years of back child support, and forget this purple crap!"

Gina's drinking and late-night crying episodes increased markedly after that. Yet Ramone concentrated on his purple figure-8 all day and until he fell asleep at night.

Purple 8 had brought Ramone closer to Maria and Victor. All of them were honor students and talked about college. Ramone was losing his jealousy over Victor and Maria. He accepted them as popular with their peers, because Maria was beautiful and Victor was both handsome and smart.

Lola and Richard's stability battled Gina's chaos. They would not let her bitterness bring down the Carillo household they had worked hard to maintain. Ramone had seen that by comparing himself to others in insane neverending negative ways took him down and made him feel worthless.

One night, not long after Ramone's fifteenth birthday, he heard his mother crying during one of her drinking binges. He went into her room and turned down the TV's volume before stepping to her bedside.

"This summer I'm going to Ocho Canyon to get a Purple 8 session from Uncle Robert," he said. "I may spend the whole summer there. I have to get away from you. You should have a session, too. Your life is about gin and pills. I don't want to see you destroy yourself."

"Well, I'm sure as hell not paying for a trip to El Centro and back!" Gina stiffened.

"Uncle Robert is paying my bus fare."

"Do me a favor, will you? When you see your father, tell him to pay you the $33,000 bucks he owes in child support!"

"I wouldn't bring it up. I'm not putting the crap between you two in my life!" Ramone yelled and stomped out of his mother's room.

Maria and Victor were nearby and heard the argument.

"Are you really going to have a session with Uncle Robert, and spend the summer there?" Maria asked.

"Yeah."

"I want to go, too," Victor whispered.

"To have a session?" his sister asked.

"To see my real dad."

Maria said, "Ramone, your mother will die if you go to spend the summer with your dad."

"She's dying anyway," he responded.

Victor and Maria knew that Ramone was right. "Could I go, too?" Maria asked Ramone.

"Why would you want to go?" Ramone asked.

"I don't want to spend all summer alone here with Gina."

Ramone nodded because he understood.

Stark

A mother in Carbonville, Illinois, encouraged her only child to finish high school so he could get a car for a graduation gift. She told her son that he could save a little money and drive away from the town that she hated as much as he did.

It worked. Warren E. Starkweather, nicknamed Stark, managed to keep his dream of one day leaving home by maintaining a 'C' average, without ever studying. He put his energy into writing about the town he hated inside thick notebooks that he hid in a box in a garage.

This garage was a safe hiding place, because it wasn't his parents' garage. It was a vacant garage next door to their house. The garage had been left standing alone on the lot after the neighbors' house was jacked up and moved away by one of those giant house-moving trucks. Since the neighbor used to work with Leroy Starkweather, the young writer's father, and Leroy had saved the man's life at work one day, the neighbor had offered the garage as free storage, until he sold his lot, which he never did.

Five notebooks had been stacked neatly inside a box in that garage over several years. Each time Stark filled another notebook, he added it to his secret collection and told himself that one day he would turn the material into a novel that would tell the world about "The Carbonville Hero of Mine Shaft 229."

Stark wrote every day. Sometimes he wrote several pages, sometimes a sentence or two. He often walked to the hills east of town, two miles from his parents' house. There he could be alone.

He knew those nameless hills better than most people around town, except for the men who mined the coal beneath them. His father was a third generation coal miner who once told his son, "What you see above ground is only the world's skin." He went on to compare it to "the smile on a politician's lyin' face." His words became even more caustic as he told his only child what he and other miners knew about the world above ground, after being under the ground for thousands of hours.

"The three building blocks of energy that made America the richest country on the earth were all black: anthracite, oil, and slaves. Today oil controls our economy, as coal and slavery once did. Evil old men with power send young men to die for that last black energy that keeps them rich. They will go kicking and screaming to their graves denying it though."

It became clear to young Stark that living with a father like that had also made his writing bitter and filled with self-pity; so, he decided that he would put more humor into his writing, or risk being labeled "stark."

Stark began watching for things to write about that were humorous, or at least funny to him. His first writing in the new yellow notebook he titled 'Funny Stuff' was about a time when he was about seven years old and his dad took him to Charlie's Barber Shop to get a haircut.

Stark wrote:

> *"I was a funny looking kid*
> *with one brown eye and one blue*
> *eye. Charlie the barber said my*
> *ears stuck out like a hyena. I had*

never seen a hyena, so I didn't think it was funny like he did. I thought my clothes were funny then, and now. They were always careworn and wrinkled; the colors were faded from repeated washings in the Carbonville hard water my mother learned to stop complaining about.

My hair looked funny. It was brown and spiked up with the green gel my dad bought at Charlie's once a year. One day while he was getting a haircut, my dad told this funny story.

"Hey, Charlie, did ya know Carbonville has the distinction of being the hometown to one of the fattest people in the world?"

Charlie grinned because he knew who my dad was talking about, but Charlie just kept cutting my dad's hair and listening and grinning as my dad went on.

"Herschel Hamburg. Fat Herschel worked in the office at Peatree Coal Company and he weighed eleven-hundred and fifty pounds of pure lard, and stood...oh...'bout six feet tall. The Company had to install a giant toilet just for Herschel's fat ass. And they had his office chair

made of solid oak, wide enough
for three people to sit on. One
day Herschel had wheels put on
his chair so he could move from
his typewriter to the phone five
feet way without getting up. Well,
the office manager, named Bud-
something, was standing behind
Herschel looking over his shoulder without Herschel knowing he
was there...and that special
chair rolled over Bud's big toe
when Herschel went to answer
his phone. You should've heard
Bud scream for his life when that
greased wheel crunched his toe.
So Bud had to wear a sandal that
fit over the cast on that toe for
six months. Bud always limped
after that and said his toenail
never grew back. He wore a
piece of rubber glued onto his
toe so his shoe didn't rub against
raw skin."

I thought that was the end
of the Herschel story, but my dad
continued.

"Well, one day in January,
fat ol' Herschel was drivin' to
work in his Bonneville when he
slid off the road and got stuck in
a ditch. Guess who came drivin'
by about that time? Yep...old Bud
with the limp. At first Bud thought

*he was gonna drive right by and
leave the big slob stuck in the
snow. But he stopped, limped
over to Herschel's rear bumper
and rocked it, with his good foot,
tryin' to get the right rear wheel
to touch down on the ground."*

*Hee, hee, hee, my dad
laughed with Charlie. I knew
Charlie had heard this story
before, about how Bud had
Herschel get out from behind the
wheel and plant his big butt on
his trunk, as Bud floored the gas
pedal with his bad toe. The car
took off down the ditch with
Herschel still on the trunk, until
the Bonneville started climbin'
out the other side.*

*I can still hear my dad and
old Charlie laughing as my dad
said, "Herschel fell off and broke
both his wrists. Old Bud and fat
Herschel, I wish I had seen it."*

Stark had figured out that his 'Funny Stuff' notebook was harder to fill, because he lacked the attitude it
took to see the world around him as humorous. His real
world at home was anything but amusing. His new attitude
had to be manufactured by positive affirmations said thousands of times a day...until he could leave Carbonville for
good.

The Trip

Maria finally convinced her mother to let her go with Victor and Ramone to visit Uncle Robert and Aunt Monica at Ocho Canyon. Maria said she wanted to be there when the boys met their father, who was now living at Blake and working in El Centro. At first, Lola said no to both of her kids, but her husband convinced her that Victor should know his biological father. Besides that, Maria and Victor had never been separated, and for Maria to be home alone with Gina was an awful thought for Lola and Richard.

By early June, three one-way bus tickets had been sent by the Ochos. Gina had acted cold to her son ever since the flare-up in her room, hence Ramone avoided her as much as possible.

"Thirteen, fourteen and fifteen," Gina reminded Lola of their ages when she came into the room to change Gina's bedding. "And too young to be on a bus that long."

But Lola wasn't fazed, reminding Gina, "As a 10-year-old girl in Mexico, I took care of six children."

Robert and Lola saw the kids off at the downtown Omaha bus terminal. Lola made sandwiches for the trip, added fruit and a gallon of bottled water to share. Each had a suitcase that they stowed in the overhead carry-on compartment, packed with enough clothes to last the summer.

They sat near the rear of the bus. Victor and Maria

sat together with Maria seated against the tall tinted window. Ramone sat across the aisle from Victor. All three of them were excited about getting out of Omaha, heading for a summer of adventure.

Victor drew the interior of the bus with a black pencil on his artist's sketch pad. Maria was lost in a romance novel she bought in the bus terminal's gift shop. Ramone was tracing his purple 8, aware of the bad feelings his mother harbored for this trip to see his father. He had kissed her goodbye and told her he'd write to her. Yet she was hurt, terribly hurt, and he felt great guilt for leaving her alone all summer.

Being so aware of his feelings was new to Ramone, and as Robert had said in his letters many times, "Any emotion you feel is generated by your mind. Own your feelings, Ramone. Go into them as deeply as you can; they will not harm you. If you disown them, they will eventually hurt your physically. Do not ignore them. Know where they come from, from the mind. And, Ramone, know that your mind is not who you are."

Their bus whined out of the city, onto 80 West. Ramone could feel his guilt growing in intensity. He resisted the urge to feed this negative emotion. Purple 8 had shown him that his mother was harming him with her negative attitudes, and he knew that his only defense was his awareness of that.

Soon anger came, fueled with despair. Again he felt intensely the guilt that had been forced on him by a mother who wallowed in terrible pain from her past. A burden she was willing to transfer to her son without thought of the damage it could do to him. Anger made him hot in the air conditioned bus. He realized that his life was being controlled by a woman who would never let him be free of her pain.

He wished he was with Robert now, instead of so many miles to go. He felt a stronger bond with his uncle than with anyone. Instinctively he knew he had to be free of his parents before their past lives destroyed his future.

He traced his purple 8 and waited for something to come, while his green eyes scanned the passengers in front of him. From the back of each stranger's head to the driver's gray uniform, he could see them all moving ahead with him, perhaps with hopes of a better life at the end of the ride through undulating prairie stretching across a cloudless blue horizon for five hundred miles.

Each stranger became a living entity, breathing with him, with hopes and dreams and problems to overcome. Could any of them be tracing a purple figure-8 with me now? he wondered. Or, could they all be going mad, like my mother, letting their minds tell them who they are in endless negative chatter?

He looked at Victor; his half-brother was lost in his sketching, a satisfied sense of skill and determination in his handsome profile. He was free to be an artist, a young man with parents who encouraged him to live, without bothering him with their problems. Victor did not need Purple 8, even though he was going to see the man who brought him into this world and then abandoned him.

"We're half-brothers with different skin, eyes, hair, and personalities. We were raised under the same roof and the same foods sustained us. Why am I the restless one and he is free to be an artist?" Ramone asked himself.

He waited for an answer; nothing came. He felt none of the old resentment he had carried during the Blake years. He saw only a brother at work with a free mind who knew he had loving parents to encourage him.

And Maria. She was free to escape into her romance novel with nothing in her past life she needed to resolve.

That's why Maria was beautiful. Many girls were beautiful, but not free of a troubled mind and uncertainties that can destroy beauty. She had gotten her wish on Flat Rock, just as Victor had. All because they had dedicated parents who adored them.

When Ramone closed his eyes, he knew that Purple 8 was all he had. His parents could never undo the damage done by that terrible incident in Las Vegas. It would always be there, as long as his mother could not walk, and that was tragic.

Late that night, they arrived in Denver for a two-hour layover. They would not change buses, so they disembarked leaving their belongings in the overhead compartments.

The Denver terminal was bigger and busier than Omaha's, with passengers and terminal employees moving about in a hundred directions.

They walked outside after waiting for Maria to use the restroom. The Denver air was thin, cool and charged with dry electricity.

Maria walked between the boys. Men stared at her when they passed by, gawking at her, their seedy rat eyes raking up and down her young body. These city vultures annoyed Ramone more than Victor, mostly because Maria and Victor were in awe of the Denver skyscrapers and not concerned with strangers. Ramone felt responsible for his younger brother and cousin, and they knew it. So they were free to let Ramone watch out for them.

Every now and then Maria or Victor would stop to point at a building or merchandise in a display window.

"Look at that dress!" Maria would shriek. Victor would engage with her over every thing she noticed, while Ramone could only trace his purple 8 in their new, bustling surroundings.

"I want to travel to a million places!" Maria declared with joy.

"Me too! And I want to draw a million places in the world," Victor laughed.

"What about you, Ramone?" Maria asked her cousin.

"What?"

"Don't you want to travel to a million places?"

"I'm traveling now," he said with a sense of the old sullenness they remembered well.

"Don't you guys wish we were going to New York or San Francisco, instead of El Centro?" Maria asked.

"Someday I'll go to those places," Victor proclaimed with certainty.

"I don't really like big cities," Ramone admitted.

"Why not?" Maria asked.

"Because places like this scare me. There's too many people. More people...more problems. I like small places."

"Like El Centro?" Victor laughed with his sister.

"You weren't so happy there," Maria reminded Ramone.

"You don't have my mother."

Victor said, "I want to see David so I can find out about my real mother."

"Maybe he'll have a picture of her that he can give you," Maria suggested.

"Yeah, that would be good," Victor agreed.

Back inside the Denver terminal, they had their picture taken together, jammed inside one of those curtained instant photo booths.

They sat in the expansive waiting area people-watching, amazed at the endless stream of characters coming and going before them.

When they boarded their bus again, they each ate a sandwich and some of the fruit that Lola had packed for them. Off they rolled, south to Colorado Springs.

They slept most of the drive to Albuquerque, where again they had a two-hour layover. This time, they changed buses with their belongings and went into the terminal's restaurant, where they enjoyed a big lunch.

They chattered happily all during their meal, and afterwards, when they stretched their legs on a walk downtown. Maria talked about the boys she liked in school, and the boys talked about girls. One, in particular, inspired spirited discussion. Maria laughed at their silliness.

"Girls don't think like guys," she told them.

"How's that?" Ramone asked.

"Girls talk about how nice and cute a guy is, but guys talk about a girl's boobies."

"Most girls are boobies!" Ramone said, and laughed with Victor.

"Girls aren't dumb enough to be turned on by Kleenex!" Maria retorted.

Hours later, the bus's climb to Flagstaff meant Phoenix was not far away. The food Lola gave them was gone. Maria had some money in her wallet, a hundred dollars that her father had given her on the way to the terminal, less what they spent for lunch in Albuquerque. The rest was for things they might need in El Centro.

Her father had said, "Let me know if you need more money. I do not want you asking my brothers or Monica for money. It's enough that they will feed you and give you a place to stay. If you need money for movies and things, call me and I will send it right away."

The ride south to Phoenix from Flagstaff, they all

agreed, was the most scenic so far. The descent from high elevation to the desert, with new scenery at every turn, reminded them of El Centro and Ocho Canyon. The bus was carrying them to a homecoming.

The final layover was in Phoenix, a three-hour stop, with more tall buildings and characters to see, while they ate a large meal in a nearby restaurant to tide them over until their early morning arrival in El Centro.

Phoenix had more homeless people than they had seen in the other cities. Dozen of careworn men sprawled on benches or crouched down in alleyways. Maria was wary of them and stayed close to Ramone.

"It must be the good weather that brings them here," Victor observed.

On a new bus on the final leg of their trip, Maria met a fourteen-year-old Latino boy from Yuma who sat in the row in front of her. They talked through the space created by his reclined seat. Like Maria, Alberto Salazar was going to be a freshman. He asked Maria what she was reading, and from then on they talked all the way to Yuma.

Maria had never taken a boy's phone number before, or given out her own. Alberto's eyes were brown like hers, his hair and skin the same color as hers. And he seemed happy with a positive personality. He talked about his big family in Yuma and how his parents had moved there from Mexico. She listened intently as he told her of his parents' hard times in Mexico, and how his father was willing to work sixteen hours a day to support his family, and recently had been promoted to vice president of a credit union.

Maria talked about her life in Omaha and the life she once had in El Centro. They liked the same music. They shared the goal of maintaining good grades in order to get a college scholarship. They agreed that they owed that much to their parents.

In Yuma, Maria stepped off the bus so she could say goodbye to Alberto. Victor and Ramone watched them from their window as they stood together chatting until Alberto's luggage was taken out of the baggage compartment of the bus. Alberto held out his right hand and she shook it, while he told her that he would call her sometime at her uncle's house.

When she boarded the bus once more, the boys teased her about her new friend, asking her if she was in love.

"If you want to keep him, you need more Kleenex," Ramone quipped.

"Yeah, to stuff in your mouth!" Maria shot back.

Maria thought about Alberto all the way to El Centro while the boys fell quiet, knowing their father would probably be there when they arrived.

Victor's left leg moved up and down fast like a piston, firing nervous pent-up energy, reminding Ramone that he was not the only one about to see a long-absent father. Like Victor, Ramone had no memory of his father, except for the verbal abuse his mother heaped on the man who had left them. Victor had been protected from Gina's tongue lashings by Lola and Richard. Ramone traced his purple 8, knowing that Victor agonized over each mile closing in on El Centro. He asked, "You anxious to meet our dad?"

Victor put down his drawing pad. "I really want to like him. I want us all to get along now and be friends." Yet Victor's leg kept moving fast.

"You seem nervous," Ramone remarked.

"I guess I am. I'd like to know about my mother, but I'm sort of afraid to ask."

"Like what?"

48

"What she was like. Every thing he knew about her. I hope he'll talk about her."

"I'd like to know those things, too."

"Why's that?"

"Because he left my mother for her."

"Are you angry about that?"

"Not like I use to be. Uncle Robert helped me with that. He told me he gave him...Dad...Purple 8 sessions in prison. I started thinkin' how maybe Purple 8 could help our family heal from what he did in Vegas."

"I don't know, Ramone. I mean, your mom said Uncle Robert's not a doctor and he has no business trying to heal people with some formula he came up with."

"The tracing has really helped me...that's all I know."

Return to Blake

David was tall and handsome, like Victor. Ramone and Maria noticed the resemblance right off when they saw the ex-con standing a head taller than Uncle Robert on the sidewalk in front of the tiny El Centro bus station. David hugged his sons; so happy to see them that he cried tears of joy.

Robert drove them in Monica's new Lincoln to have breakfast at a pancake house. David's eyes were clear and attentive, like Robert's, as he asked the boys about their school and their lives in Omaha. David was open about the mistakes he made that put him behind bars, saying that he was a new man now, and that his new job selling used cars in El Centro was the fresh start he needed.

When Maria was teased and forced by the boys to talk about Alberto, she found the men nonjudgmental and genuinely interested about her new friend from Yuma.

After a two-hour breakfast flavored with honest conversation, they headed for Ocho Canyon. On the way, the kids wanted to stop at Blake. Before they got out of the car in front of their old home, Robert explained that he had rented Blake to David and that Richard did not want Gina to know. The kids understood, yet David told them frankly, "Gina has bad feelings for me...which I understand. Richard wants to help me without upsetting her. To keep the peace, I hope you can all understand that Gina doesn't need to know I'm living here."

Blake was sparsely furnished, with only a couch in the main room. A radio played Mexican music on an unfinished end table in the kitchen. David laughed and admitted, "I bought the table at a swap meet for five bucks."

He showed the kids his room, Lola and Richard's old bedroom, which now had a twin bed and an open closet that displayed the ex-con's humble wardrobe for work, a few white shirts with ties and two pairs of black slacks.

The kids checked out their old rooms. Ramone went into his mother's old room, alone. He stood there looking at the dust rings that revealed the space where her bed had been. Her room was full of ghosts. He imagined her there on her bed, her thinning red hair on her clean, white pillowcase. The room seemed clouded with cigarette smoke; he could smell it still.

Guilt for leaving her alone in Omaha nearly overwhelmed him. This was the first time he had been away from her and it brought up old pain that had been buried since he last lived here. Images crowded in on him and made him nauseous. To calm himself, he traced his purple 8, then left his mother's room before anyone saw him.

He went into his old room, but he could hear her crying again in the night, though he traced faster and faster, standing motionless with his eyes closed. A tear rolled down his cheek and splashed hard onto his shoe; it made him see her lifeless legs with scaling red skin that would never walk again. At the sound of footsteps behind him, he wiped his eyes and tried to hide all evidence of his emotional return to Blake.

He felt a tall, quiet presence standing behind him in the doorway.

"This was your room," David said softly.

"Yeah."

"And your mother's room was on the end." Ramone nodded without turning to face his father.

"Robert told me. When I first moved in, I had him show me your rooms."

They stood in an awkward silence until David stepped forward and put his hands on the boy's shoulder.

"I'll bet this place brings back memories for you." Another nod.

"Is there anything you want to tell me, or ask me, Ramone?"

His head was bowed low when he told his father that he wished the accident had never happened.

"I do, too. It was the worst time in my life."

"Why'd you leave her there?"

"I was scared. I thought she was dead. It was wrong."

"If you had helped her then...she might not be so angry at you."

"Maybe. But I ran like a coward. I've regretted that everyday since. Can you forgive me for that?"

Ramone felt as if he was strangling, gasping for air.

David crumbled to his knees and slumped over as if he were ill.

"Ramone," he begged, "we've both got stuff to get rid of here. Please tell me how you feel. I want to help you and Victor. This Purple 8 stuff has given me hope that I can make things up to all of you."

Fear of this man he really didn't know or trust shut Ramone down. It was all so pathetic to him, how this man, supposed to be his father, was here now, in his old room, and so pitiful and desperate to rid himself of burdens. It made Ramone want to withhold forgiveness, to punish the man who had made him a prisoner with his mother for as long as he could remember.

When no words came from his son, David blurted, "I didn't tell you everything about that time in Vegas. I was dealing blackjack at a casino. I'd been stealing from the house for some time. I know I was lucky to get away with it for so long. The night of the accident I had stolen about two grand and was going to leave town with Victor's mother. The thought of the police finding me with the money...that's why I didn't stop to help your mother. Plus I was scared that she might be dead. That's why I got you and brought you here. I knew that Richard would take good care of you."

"Victor's mother, why didn't you take her with you when you left Vegas?"

"I figured why bring her into my mess when she's going to have a kid. I'm very thankful that your mother got Richard and Lola to adopt Victor. Now I'm beside myself. I have no clue what to do to make up to Gina what I'm responsible for. Your mother is very proud and stubborn. That was what made her act so crazy and jump on my car like she did. Ramone, there's something I have to tell you."

Just then, Victor and Maria appeared in the doorway. They balked when they saw David turning to sit on the floor.

Ramone had to get out of the room, the walls were closing in on him. He pushed past Victor and Maria, then ducked out the front door.

Robert called the two younger children over to sit with him on the sofa, aware of the scene they had witnessed. He explained to them that David had many things to get off his heart and that both his sons would see someday that their father had always cared about them. Now Victor had new thoughts about what he would ask his father.

Robert left the two kids and went into Ramone's room where he found his brother seated on the floor holding his face in his hands. Robert sat down near his brother and pulled his hands away from his tearstained face.

"David, it's good that you are letting go of your grief. But remember to trace your purple 8 to keep your mind from holding onto the pain. That's how the mind wants things. It wants to destroy any inner peace that you claim." David nodded, showing that he understood, as his brother continued talking to him softly, "What was it that your mind revealed that released this pain in your body? Do you remember exactly what the images were?"

"Yes. I saw Ramone as a baby the time I went with Gina to the doctor; we all got flu shots. I held him while the needle went into his little arm. And his little hand squeezed my hand when the needle hurt him. I remember how his eyes were begging me to protect him from the pain. That image always comes to me when I need a good cry. Not just in prison, either. So, when I walked into his room, I suddenly realized all the times he must've needed to squeeze my hand, but I wasn't there for him. I feel terrible guilt for not being a father to the boys."

Robert put his powerful hands on his brother's tense shoulders. "You can do nothing about the past that will change one thing that your boys went through. If you don't learn to eliminate all this guilt—it will destroy you and any future you may have with your sons."

Yet what Robert told his brother when they helped each other to their feet, were the most insightful words David had ever heard from anyone.

"Those boys can't forgive you until they see that you have forgiven yourself."

"Can I get a session soon?"

"Tomorrow," Robert smiled.

More Purple Crap

At Ocho Canyon, Monica and her niece talked late into the night on the back patio while sipping ginger tea. Maria told her aunt that she was happy with her life in Omaha. She liked her school and the friends she'd made. There were many places to shop and more things to do. And her family was doing better financially. Then she blushed as she told Monica that she had met a cute boy on the bus in Phoenix.

"His name is Alberto Salazar. He lives with his family in Yuma. He's fourteen...five months older than me."

"Yuma! That's not far away! Maybe you will see him this summer," Monica smiled.

"Maybe. I gave him the phone number here. I have his number, too. Should I call him?"

"If you want. But wait a few days. Boys like to be the first to call."

The boys shared the queen-size bed in one of the two guest bedrooms. Both boys were restless after their uncle told them that they could have a session with their father on Flat Rock the next night. As they lay together on the comfortable mattress, the pearl moon shone through the open window.

"What happened in your room today?" Victor asked.

"Oh, I was into my head how pathetic my mother's life has been. And now I'm here and she's alone back there."

"Maybe the session will help you." Victor paused. "Gina calls it purple crap."

"I know," Ramone laughed.

"Do you think I should try it tomorrow?"

"It's up to you."

"What were you talking about in your room?"

"He was tellin' me how he stole money from his job in Vegas. That's the real reason he left my mom. He was pretty scared. I couldn't feel sorry for him when I thought of how my mom is in pain all the time."

"Yeah. Did he say he was sorry for what he did?"

"Pretty much."

"Do you think he'll tell me about my mother?"

"Probably. If it bothers you, you should ask him."

"Yeah. I think I will."

"Tomorrow's the perfect time...on Flat Rock."

"I guess," Victor sighed.

Again, his brother's foot was pumping nervously, just like it had on the bus. "Would you stop that shaking?" Ramone muttered.

"Sorry. I do that when I'm nervous."

"What are you nervous about?"

"I guess, finding out things about my real mom...how she was...why she gave me up."

"You should trace purple 8 in your head...like we did that time on Flat Rock. I've been doin' it most every day since then. Nothin' bothers me when I do it. Try it, Victor!"

After a few minutes spent imagining a huge, purple figure-8, Victor couldn't see what good it was doing. Maybe Gina was right, he thought.

56

"Were you thinking of anything when you did it?"

Victor shook his head no.

"That's the point! It keeps your mind quiet!" Ramone laughed.

Return to Flat Rock

David and the boys skipped breakfast, because Robert told them it would enhance the session if they fasted for the day. They drank Monica's herbal tea, which would empty their colons in twelve hours. The girls served them tea all day, which kept the two bathrooms busy.

That afternoon, Alberto called Maria. They talked for an hour. When she got off the phone she announced to her aunt that Alberto was catching a bus to El Centro the next morning because he wanted to spend the day with her.

"He said we could see a movie. Can you take me to the bus station to meet him?"

"Yes! I have to do some shopping. I can pick you up afterward."

"Great! I'll call him. He said his bus arrives at 12:15."

Monica thought about calling Lola and Richard to tell them about their daughter's date, but decided not to, when Robert suggested that the boys go to the movies with them. Maria was okay with the boys going, as long as she didn't have to sit with them.

At nightfall, Robert led the way into Ocho Canyon by flashlight, carrying a five-foot-tall hickory walking stick to ward off snakes. David trailed the boys, also wary of snakes that time of year.

Victor was wary of other things; he'd made a mental

list of questions he wanted to ask David. Yet, now, he was confused about asking any of the things on his list.

David felt just as anxious as Victor, for he too had things he wanted to say to his son before he went back to work in the morning.

The purple stain in a figure-8 on Flat Rock glowed in the moon's light. Right away Robert passed around a canteen filled with his formula. He could see that his nephews were anxious, but each took a sip of the chalky, sweet, lavender liquid. Oddly, it seemed to dry the tongue.

"Ramone and Victor, each of you sit inside one of the loops. David, you sit here." He pointed to a spot between the boys.

Robert sat across from his brother where the figure-8 crossed. With brothers facing brothers, Robert controlled the passing of the canteen, as the chirping of desert insects filled the night air with incredible intensity, reverberating from the canyon's looming walls glowing silver-red in the moonlight.

Robert had been waiting for this moment ever since his wayward brother left Las Vegas. To have the sons here with their father, with no time restrictions on them— the stage was set for real progress.

Victor's foot thumped fast until his third swallow from the canteen, whereupon he vomited white froth off to his side onto the flat rock.

"That's good, Victor. It won't harm you. You are eliminating toxins from your body."

Then Robert told them all to visualize a purple 8 and trace the shape.

Before long, David, then Ramone, each heaved onto the flat surface a foam that spread, snapping on the cool rock.

"Close your eyes and stay with your purple 8.

When stuff comes out, say out loud what you saw!" Robert commanded as his hawkish brown eyes roamed from Victor to Ramone and to his brother.

David's violent vomiting startled the boys, and then his guttural outburst, "I saw you boys growing up hating me! It was awful!"

Next, Ramone heaved a fountain of foam that ran down his chin.

"What, Ramone?" his uncle asked softly.

"I saw myself killing my mother...smothering her with her pillow..."

"Where, Ramone?" Robert asked.

"At Blake...in her room! I wanted to end her pain!" He heaved again.

Victor opened his eyes. His uncle said, "Close your eyes, Victor. Stay with your tracing; see the purple 8. Nothing here will hurt you."

Robert knew from experience that his nephew was frightened of an image he didn't want to confront.

Then, Victor exploded a gush of foam onto his lap.

"That's good, Victor! What did you see?"

"I saw my mother giving me away...without a fight! She was glad to be rid of me!" he cried.

Then it was David's turn. "It was me, Victor! I told your mother I had a family! She said she would kill herself and you, too, if I didn't marry her! I left her. I didn't want any more kids! I wasn't even a father to Ramone! When I found out Richard had adopted you...at first I wished she had killed herself, so I didn't have to live with two sons on my conscience! When I was in Mexico, I drove a half ton of Mexican weed up to Tucson in six trips. I didn't care if I got busted. They paid me a hundred grand, altogether. I buried my share of the money before I was caught on my last run. It's still there...for you boys and for Gina. I wanted to give the three of you something. Nothing I could say would ever change the past, but that money at least says I want to make things up to you...all of you."

"Tell them the rest," Robert instructed his brother.

"In prison I got word there was a contract out on my life, because of the money I stole in Vegas. I owed them ten grand. I called my ex-boss as soon as I got paroled, and he said he wanted his money in a few days. I drove to the place where I hid the money, dug it up, and wired ten grand to the casino in Vegas. The rest is for you boys and Gina."

"All of you...open your eyes and keep tracing!" Robert ordered.

Ramone and Victor sat wide-eyed, looking at each other, while David sat staring at his brother.

"Ramone, Victor...will this money help you forgive your father?"

"I don't want it," Ramone stated firmly. "I forgive him anyway."

"Victor?" Robert queried.

"I think all the money should go to Gina. I forgive him, too."

"Will Gina take the money?" Robert asked Ramone.

"I don't know. She always wanted child support. I don't think she'd take it knowing it was drug money."

"Then don't tell her," Victor said.

"I want her to know it came from me," David said.

"I have an idea," Robert smiled. "David can send a thousand dollars a week to Gina, telling her it's from selling cars. And in two years or so she'll have all the money. What do you think?"

All of them agreed to keep secret the plan to pay Gina. Robert swore that he would not even tell his wife. Father and sons were starting over in a conspiracy that would help David's greatest victim.

On the way back to the house, David related to Victor all that he knew about his mother. It was pretty much what Lola and Richard had always told their son, that she had been very young and not ready to be a mother.

First Date

Just before show time, Victor and Ramone sat in the back row of The Jupiter eating popcorn and feeling good about last night's incredible session on Flat Rock. Both boys were tickled, imagining how surprised Gina was going to be when she received her first money order for a thousand dollars. David had mailed the money enclosed in a letter that morning. Both Ramone and Victor had written Gina a letter after they returned home last night, as well.

Ramone wrote that his father was doing well selling cars and wanted to pay her back for nonsupport all those years. He wrote that he had told David his mother could really use some money. And he told her he missed her and that he was enjoying his visit at Ocho Canyon.

David wrote his ex-wife about his success selling cars, telling her he had always wanted to help her and Ramone, and that he regretted not being around to see Ramone grow up.

When the lights in the theater dimmed for previews, the boys watched Maria and her date take their seats in the middle of the theater. Maria waved at them before she sat down next to Alberto. This was her first date with a boy she admired, and she was very nervous.

As the couple shared a box of popcorn Maria was still savoring the emotions singing within her as she met Alberto's bus at the tiny El Centro bus station. His wide smile made her heart lurch. Then he became more cautious as they walked to The Jupiter with Ramone and Victor a few steps ahead of them. Maria explained that the boys were along to chaperone.

Alberto behaved as a perfect gentleman, giving Maria a wrapped present as they strolled toward the theater. "Open it now," he said, showing her again his joyful grin.

As she opened the gift, the boys kept glancing back to see what it was. When they saw that it was a box of chocolates, they stopped in their tracks. Maria offered the box to her hungry chaperones, and half the chocolates vanished in an instant.

Midway through the movie, Alberto put his arm around Maria and kept it there until the final credits ended and the lights came on. The boys waited in the back row for the couple to get up, but the couple sat there talking.

"I told my parents I met you on the bus," Alberto said.

"What did they say?"

"Not much. They think I'm crazy to take a bus all the way to El Centro to see you."

"I think it's nice," Maria blushed and feared the boys could now hear every word in the quiet theater.

"I wish you lived in Yuma," he said.

"We could be pen pals," she suggested.

"I'm not much of a writer. I could call you...even when you go back to Omaha."

"That would be nice."

The boys began mocking them just when she thought Alberto was going to kiss her. It seemed that they had thought the same thing. She started to laugh when the guys smacked their lips loudly behind them. Alberto surprised her when he took her hand firmly in his and led her past her guardians without a glance in their direction.

Maria and Alberto talked in front of the theater entrance while the guys stood fifty feet away waiting for Monica to pick them up. Alberto still had a couple of hours left before his bus departed for Yuma.

When Monica arrived she treated them all to a late lunch at a fast-food spot off I-8. Monica made her nephews sit with her in a booth far enough away from Maria and her date to give them some privacy.

Alberto told Maria, "I want you to send me a photo. Without the chaperones!" They laughed.

He teased, "I'll send you my picture, but it'll be ugly."

Maria giggled. "Not as ugly as those two!" she said, pointing at Ramone and Victor.

"I think you're the most beautiful girl I've ever seen in my life," he said, "I hope I can see you again soon. If not, I want us to promise to see each other again, to meet somewhere. Okay?"

"Yes."

"Let's pick a place, somewhere we can agree to meet when we're older, without your bodyguards." He smiled. "I know! How about in front of The Jupiter?"

"Okay."

"Great! We'll meet again someday in front of the theater. Just the two of us."

She waved goodbye to him from the sidewalk as his bus pulled away. Her mouth was tingling from the quick kiss he planted there just moments ago. She thought of the day she would see him again in front of The Jupiter. She'd be older, wearing a new dress, one she picked out just for him. He'd be taller and no one would be there to dim his smile.

As she walked to Monica's waiting car she wondered if any of them had seen the kiss. They hadn't. Or else one of the boys would have teased her, for sure. They didn't.

A Drive Before Walking

David did very well selling used cars at El Centro Auto. He was fluent in Spanish and his boss was a top notch mechanic who guaranteed that the vehicles would run without major repairs for one year, or the repairs were on him. The commissions David made were a blessing to him because he didn't have to touch the money he intended to give Gina.

Saturday morning, David was surprised when his boss picked him up for work in a vintage, 1960, black Ford Falcon that he'd been working on. He told his star salesman that the car was his as long as he continued to work for him, and paid for his own liability insurance.

This provided the freedom David had been longing for. Now he could leave the lot without waiting for a ride from his boss. Since he had the next day off, he called his sons and told them that he wanted to take the boys for a drive in his new car. He promised he would give them a driving lesson on the reservation, just like his father had done for him.

All day the boys talked about their driving lesson while they learned about the Ocho's thriving Purple 8 business among Native American customers in California. If their uncle wasn't treating a native local at the clinic on the reservation, he and Monica were filling orders at home in their kitchen. Robert measured and filled purple capsules with the powdered formula, while Monica addressed the little packages. The next morning a van would pick up the orders to be delivered.

Ramone was more interested in the business than Victor. He could see that it was an easy way to make money, and even if the other kids didn't know it, he was the heir to Ocho Canyon.

Victor was more interested now in photography than in drawing. Time spent in his father's projection room at work had changed his perspective on visual arts. "I'd like to make a documentary film," he told his brother.

"About what?"

"I don't know yet, but it sure beats drawing something that nobody cares about."

"Cameras are expensive. Maybe if you ask my mom, she'll buy you a camera with some of the money she's getting now."

"You think so?" Victor's eyes widened.

"If she knows you really want to learn, she might. What else would she do with all that cash all of a sudden? Ask her when we get back."

Sunday, David picked up the boys in his Falcon and let them drive around the dirt roads surrounding Ocho Canyon. They had a great time, especially David, who was thrilled to finally be there when his boys learned something for the first time.

After dinner, when David left the house, the boys and Maria called home. Gina was happy to hear from Ramone. She said she was surprised and thrilled to get the money from David. When her excited son told her about his driving lesson, she had nothing negative to say. Ramone believed that the money, the symbol that his father regretted the past, had cut through some of her bitterness.

When Lola and Richard finished talking to the kids, Gina called out to them from her room. When they walked through the bedroom door, they were stunned to see Gina standing, grasping the walker she had never tried to use before. To their amazement, she managed to take a couple of baby steps before they rushed to her side.

She said, "I'll need your help. I have to quit smoking and drinking, and get off the pain pills. And Purple 8, I want to take the capsules Monica sent me."

Legacy Revealed

Victor, Ramone and David had three sessions with Robert on Flat Rock that summer. Each session brought father and sons closer. The boys began calling David "Dad" and that made him very happy. Most of their good feelings toward their father stemmed from the fact that he had kept his word and sent Gina a thousand dollars a week, for eight weeks in a row.

Ramone and Victor became closer than ever; it was Maria who noticed how much their friendship had grown over the summer. "You were friends," she said. "Now, you are brothers."

Maria was blossoming into a real beauty after spending so much time with her sophisticated aunt. Maria had no interest in Purple 8; unlike her brothers, she had not drunk the juice of the mysterious blue cactus that grew only on her family's land.

One Sunday, Robert and David agreed that both boys should be told about the Carillo legacy. David did not think that Gina had told Ramone about his birthright claim to Ocho Canyon. Both Robert and David believed the legacy had been created hundreds of years ago to ensure that a Carillo male remained at Ocho Canyon. David did not want Ramone to make the same mistakes he had; he wanted the boys to work together, even if only one of them was in line to inherit Ocho Canyon.

With five days left before they returned to the Midwest, Robert took the boys for a long morning walk behind the canyon's walls where the blue cactus lived.

He told them about the family legacy, everything he knew. They listened to their uncle's words with rapt attention in this place where the blue cactus dotted the desert landscape around them. When he was through talking, he asked each boy questions concerning the legacy.

"What do you think about this, Ramone?"

"Does this mean that when I get married I can live here?"

"Yes, if Monica and I don't want to live here anymore."

"Where would you live?"

"Anywhere we want." Robert smiled at Ramone.

"But what about the blue cactus and your formula?"

"It will be your formula, because you will have taken it over as I did from my father."

Robert led them over to a mature blue cactus with huge, spiny arms entwined in multiple figure-8s. He pointed to the base of the cactus.

"There are not many of these older blue cactus that produce the ripe juice for the formula. The younger ones are not ready. I can only use what is ready, and it is enough to sustain my needs. In ten years, or less, there will be a big harvest of the mature ones, bigger than any time in Ocho Canyon's history. There will be plenty of juice for the formula to be marketed to the general public as a diet supplement. I can't do it alone."

Robert asked Victor, "How does this legacy stuff make you feel?"

"I'm happy for Ramone...if he wants to live out here. It's too isolated for me. I like cities. Ramone has always been more interested in Purple 8, he traces much more than I do. It just bores me."

Even then Ramone was tracing, seeing himself living at the rim of the canyon some day.

Victor continued, "If Ramone decides he's not interested in the life here, then I'm next in line for it?

"That's right. Either way I believe that brothers should help each other reach their dreams, even if those dreams are different. Think about it. Work together and support each other."

Mental Baggage and a Surprise

There were no sad goodbyes when they boarded their bus for Omaha. David and Robert stood waving until the bus was out of view. On their walk to their vehicles, the brothers knew that this had been a good summer for all of them.

"I'm already looking forward to next summer," David told his brother.

Maria sat alone next to a window. Ramone and Victor sat together across the aisle with Ramone taking the window seat.

Their sister was thinking of Alberto and how she hadn't been able to talk to him since their date at The Jupiter. She had called him once and left a message with his mother, but he never returned her call. Earlier in the day, she resisted the urge to call him to let him know when her bus was stopping in Yuma.

The image of their reunion at The Jupiter, sweet thoughts of how it would be when they saw each other again, had faded from her daily musings. Monica had consoled her, mentioning the many boys who would come and go in her life, before she met the right one. "And the same for him," her aunt had said.

And yet Maria wanted to see him again, to see how she felt about him. Aunt Monica was probably right.

Alberto must have met someone, she told herself as their bus picked up I-8 and headed east.

Maria read all the way to Phoenix; she walked alone through the crowded Phoenix terminal during their layover. This was the place where they had met. Now, it seemed silly to her. Even the books she loved to read were about lost love after chance encounters. "Another romance novel, that's what Alberto Salazar is for me," she sighed.

The return trip to Omaha seemed much longer for Maria. The boys played cards most of the time and napped often. Maria read and brooded about her lost love. Ramone commented on her mood when they reached Denver, telling her, "It's only mental baggage. Let it go, before it owns you."

At the Omaha terminal, the trio stepped off the bus and froze in gape-jawed wonder upon seeing Gina standing behind an aluminum walker with Lola and Richard flanking her. Gina's red hair had been cut short; the style looked good on her. Richard motioned for the kids to stay put as Gina dipped her pronounced Irish chin, pursed her lips, and managed to slide each shoe forward as few inches. Each step was a miracle for the family as Richard and Lola patiently crept alongside her.

The kids watched Gina lift the four rubber-tipped legs of the walker with no apparent strain, for her upper body was strong. Her incredible will was moving her lower body forward ever so slowly. That was Gina's place, her mind; it had always been her strength, and served her now as she focused her sights on Ramone, inching closer.

Ramone was moved by her courage, not by the raw physical feat performed by his mother, but rather, the way she faced the world right now, as a fighter who refused to quit. Her appearance was such a contrast to the pale woman with unkempt hair and no makeup that he left only eleven weeks before, he almost didn't recognize her. She wore a whimsical smirk lined neatly with red lipstick that made her son want to find out what she'd been up to.

Gina stepped up to her son. Even then, he kept his purple 8 swirling, not letting dammed guilt for leaving her run rampant and ruin this surprise.

She stood before the three kids and raised her head to look directly at the young Carillos.

"Remember this, all of you: Sometimes it's the lack of money that's the root of all evil. David has now given me the means to do things for myself, and to begin saving for your education. That has made all the difference. I hated him for not helping, and I hated myself."

Lola and Richard were relieved to see that their decision to let Maria and Victor return to Ocho Canyon had been a good one. On the ride home, Maria told them about Alberto and their chaperoned date at The Jupiter. She also explained that it was the last time she had seen or spoken to Alberto.

"But now I'm over him. He probably met someone else," she said with fake cheeriness.

Gina said, "It's okay to be disappointed."

Victor was still thinking of asking Gina to help him buy a digital video camera, because he knew Richard would make him wait until he'd saved his own money. So, Victor decided to research cameras and choose the best before he approached Gina.

Seated in back with Victor and Maria, Ramone continued tracing, even though he was happy to see his mother riding on the front passenger seat. His mind was on something else. Ramone's image of living at Ocho Canyon when he married had been clear ever since he learned about his legacy. Still, he recalled what David had told him, "The dream of Ocho Canyon may fade, as it did with me. Then came a time I wished I'd held that image, instead of the path I took. But Ocho Canyon has to be something you want, not what anyone else wants for you. Nobody ever knows what's best for someone else. The harvest is like any great idea...it sounds like Paradise...but working it out is hell."

Sixteen and Fast...With a Plan

Ramone found out early in his sophomore year in Omaha that he was the fastest guy in his class. In P. E. class just before the weather turned cold, 10.2 seconds in the hundred was the third fastest time any sophomore ever ran in the school's history. The junior varsity football coach tried to talk Ramone into joining the team a month into the season, but Ramone had no interest in football.

Since the JV football coach was also the varsity track coach, he tried to give the sprinter a few tips for building his leg strength in the school's weight room. Ramone just nodded and said rather sullenly, "That doesn't interest me." The coach saw that there was no pushing Ramone Carillo; the kid was way too independent, which is why the coach thought he was suited for track, where Ramone would be racing alone, against his own record.

Their summer at Ocho Canyon had been good for Ramone and Victor's confidence. Victor was gathering information on cameras. Richard had advised his son to go to the University of Nebraska's media center and check out the equipment the college students used there, which he did.

Ramone's legacy motivated him to learn fast and forego pursuits of glory on the track. He believed his future would be secure once he married. Every bit of confusion and doubt he harbored about his life had vanished in the swirling purple of his figure-8, as his uncle and father had said it would.

David had said to his sons, "Robert told me about his perfected Purple 8 formula when I first went into prison. I wasn't allowed to take any, but I traced purple 8 nearly every waking minute to keep myself from being depressed."

Now Ramone focused on the dream David had placed in his keeping—for the future—for the Carillo family. His father had said, "If you two are smart, you will open markets to reach the public when the crop of blue cacti matures in the new century. It will be a gold mine. You two should come back every summer to pick Robert's brain about Purple 8. Find out all you can, because you can both be rich when you're still young. There's no better way to live!"

Day and night, while tracing whenever he could, Ramone summoned his controlled mind to produce ideas that would bring him great wealth from the harvest...without getting married.

Then the answer came to him one cold Saturday morning as he ambled beside his mother's walker on an Omaha sidewalk. Gina was moving at the speed of a turtle, headed to the bank to deposit her weekly money order from David. She usually went alone, and it took nearly two hours for her to make the four-block-long roundtrip, but she wanted to do it—in order to push her body to keep moving.

On their walk, Ramone talked about the summer and how he was looking forward to returning next year. His mother listened without the usual harsh judgments and negative labels she used to attach to actions and people. Now her energy focused on each single step, for the pain was excruciating in her damaged hips, the lowest place on her body where she had unhindered sensation.

In the bank, Ramone noticed the security camera mounted up high on the wall behind the tellers. In one split second, he could see the future unfolding.

When Gina inched up to the teller's window and handed the teller her deposit slip, Ramone saw that it was filled out for $950.00 with $50.00 cash back. "I'd like a twenty-dollar bill and thirty singles please," she told the teller.

She gave Ramone the twenty and stuffed the singles in her front pocket. Every morning, when Lola had the kids' lunch sacks ready and sitting on the kitchen table, Gina put two bucks inside each sack.

On the return walk home from the bank, Ramone said, "Mom, I'd like to buy a video camera for Victor. He's really interested in making films. If you would consider taking one of Uncle Robert's sessions, I know you would make progress much faster." He paused, then blurted, "And Victor could document your progress on a video!"

"What brought this on?" she asked while creeping down the sidewalk.

"I want to market Purple 8 and maybe live at Ocho Canyon."

"Did your father tell you about Ocho Canyon?"

"And Uncle Robert. He said there's going to be a huge crop of blue cactus within the next ten years."

"Are you sure that Victor wants a video camera?"

"Yes!"

"Have him tell me how much it is and I'll give him the money."

"Thanks, Mom. We'll pay you back."

"No...it's a gift."

"Will you take Uncle Robert's session?"

"I'm almost ready for a session," she admitted.

"I've been taking his formula with my meds."

"Mom, that's great! I'm pretty sure you'll be able to walk on your own if you trust Purple 8."

"We'll see. Did you have a session?"

"Yes...with Dad and Victor. It was incredible, Mom...the stuff I was holding onto. And I keep an image of a purple 8 in my mind most of the day. It helps me focus on what's important."

"If it works for you, do it. Do you and Victor call David Dad now?"

"Yeah. Calling him David just didn't feel right."

"I can see that."

"You don't mind do you, Mom?"

"No, I understand it," she smiled.

At the end of the block, stepping down to the street from the sidewalk was the most painful part of her walk. She pursed her lips and eased herself down backwards with her walker on the sidewalk. Ramone held back; he could tell she wanted to do it without help. The steps to the other sidewalk were slow, with traffic moving cautiously around them. Going up the other curb was even more difficult for her, lifting the walker onto the sidewalk, then stepping upwards. But she laughed in good spirits about her infirmity, saying to her son, "My body feels like it's two hundred years old. Winter is the worst time for me."

"Why don't you move back to El Centro where it's warmer?"

"No, Richard and Lola are happy here."

"I would move with you, if you want."

"No, this is our home now."

Victor was sitting on his twin bed in the boys' bedroom, listening to a CD, when Ramone told him that his mother would buy a camera for him.

"I said we wanted to document her recovery if she had a Purple 8 session with Uncle Robert. She said she would, Vic!"

"Really?"

"Yes! I couldn't believe it. She said yes without any argument."

"That's amazing."

"I know. But if you could film her recovery, I know we can market it somehow."

"That's a good idea, Mone."

"Figure out what camera you want, and how much, and she'll pay for it."

"That's great news! At school there's this teacher who shoots the varsity games. I know he can help me. He knows everything about cameras and he said I can get a digital camera at a good price, because he buys stuff for the school and gets a good deal."

"Ya know, Victor, I think we both ought to trace purple 8s like Uncle Robert keeps saying we should."

"Mone, you're into that more than I am. I get bored with it."

"I know, but since my mom and I will be doing it, I think you should, too. That would make our documentary more real and truthful, coming from all of us. Ya know what I mean?"

"Maybe...I guess."

"Do it more often is all I'm sayin'...okay?"

"Okay."

"I'm going to work on a plan to market Purple 8. Any ideas you have...let me know."

Victor replied, "You're gonna be the salesman, Bro. I'm the film maker. My place is gonna be in the cutting room."

A Family Project

That November, Maria spent time at night creating a script for Ramone, questions he could ask Gina at her bedside at the beginning of Purple 8, the title of their first documentary.

Victor had been using his new digital camera at school, getting help from students who had the same kind of camera.

Ramone had called Uncle Robert to tell him about the documentary, and that Gina wanted a session with him. "That's incredible news, Ramone!" his uncle had said on the phone. "I can fly to Omaha anytime you're ready."

"She's ready now."

"How about Thanksgiving weekend when you're out of school?"

"Okay, but we want you in the documentary to talk about Purple 8."

"I'd love to! With Gina as an example, this could really open some closed minds."

"Is there enough formula to sell now?"

"Yes. It's not FDA approved, but not illegal to sell on the reservation. There's not enough supply to really go gangbusters until the plants mature in five years or so. But Ramone, there is enough to get something going. I'm not very good about marketing to the public. I'm good at one on one."

"So, around 2008, there will be much more?"

"About then."

Ramone chuckled. "That's funny: Purple 8 in 2008. Can we make money from the documentary?"

"That's an interesting idea. We'll have to see what we can come up with. I want it to be a family project."

Robert was so excited after Ramone's phone call that he drove over to Blake and waited outside until his brother got home from work. When David parked his Falcon by the front door Robert leaned out of his truck and told him about Ramone and Victor's documentary, along with Gina's willingness to have a session.

"I guess maybe the money helped," David told his brother.

"Just keep sending a grand a week, like you have. And she's walking now!"

"Really?"

"Ramone told me she's using a walker. Can you believe that?"

David nodded. "That is amazing." But then he became quiet.

"What is it, brother?" Robert asked, as David unlocked the front door to Blake and they stepped inside.

"I was remembering how good it was with Gina before we got married...all the fun we used to have."

"Have you been visualizing your 8?"

"Yeah. The other day I was closing this deal on a Bronco, about a nine hundred dollar commission for me. Suddenly the guy backed out and left. But I started tracing my 8. The lost deal didn't even phase me. It was like it never happened. Then I realized I was changing the way I react to things, because the boys have forgiven me and are back in my life. And now it looks like Gina's finally taking care of herself. I feel like I'm getting a new start. Walking out of prison I wanted two things to happen: I wanted the boys to forgive me, and I wanted to see Gina happy again. Money...it's funny...I lost her because I loved money...and now giving it away is bringing her back."

"Money, or love?" Robert asked.

Purple 8

Victor bought a quality microphone for their first documentary. Ramone was ready to ask the questions. They had rehearsed it many times in Gina's room. From her orthopedic bed, dressed in a v-neck sweater that was the color of an azure afternoon sky, her red hair looked stunning. Gina Carillo was ready to give the performance of her life.

Gina knew that this was the beginning of a five-year journey to build the wealth that David had told her about long ago on Flat Rock, a legacy she also wanted for Ramone. David had explained that the harvest of blue cactus reached its peak about every hundred years. Ramone had said the time was near, probably in 2008.

Robert was a healer and herbalist; David and Richard were not interested in marketing the blue cactus. Maybe Ramone, she thought. That was her motivation now, to help sell Purple 8 for her son, so he could live at Ocho Canyon and not struggle.

Maria was the family member who cared the least about Purple 8 and the Carillo legacy that promised great wealth for the family. She just wanted Gina to walk again, not only for her sake—for Ramone. Her cousin would be able to live an independent life only if his mother could fend for herself. Gina needed a life free of pain, she deserved one.

The *Purple 8* interview began with the questions Maria had scripted and Ramone had memorized. Victor's lens panned Gina's room first, then a close-up of Gina's bedside table holding rows of prescription bottles. A close-up of Gina, her red lipstick lined perfectly by Maria and her teeth recently whitened by a dentist.

"It's November 19th, 2003. This is my mother, Gina Carillo. She's 34 years old and was injured in a car accident about fifteen years ago. The accident left her paralyzed from her waist down."

Now Victor's lens focused on Ramone and zoomed in on the purple pill between his fingers.

"My mother began taking this purple pill last summer, along with her prescription medication. What did you notice right away?" Ramone asked Gina.

The camera pulled back to reveal Gina as she answered frankly, "It gave me more energy, no doubt about that. I was still taking my medications, as I do today, but back then I smoked and drank alcohol...so I wasn't feeling very good about myself. Last summer I quit smoking and drinking and it was easier than I ever imagined. Then the new energy allowed me to get up and try to walk with my walker."

In the next shot, Maria and Ramone helped Gina out of bed. The camera followed Gina's unassisted steps as she walked around her room.

Victor stopped filming, and Gina sat on her bed again. With the camera rolling once more, he went back to Ramone.

"Soon the creator of the purple pill, my uncle Robert Carillo, will arrive from Southern California to explain the origin of the natural healing agents in his formula. You will see him give my mother a treatment that will clear her body of toxins."

They spent hours reviewing what they had shot with Victor's digital camera. It looked good to them. Tomorrow they would shoot Gina in motion outdoors, before a forecasted snowfall arrived.

This was the beginning. The boys were excited about their documentary. And Gina was about to embark on the hardest test of all.

In five days, Monica and Robert would arrive. Before Robert could give her the Purple 8 session, she had to stop taking her prescription pain medication and sleeping pills. With Ramone to support her, she began the ordeal of withdrawal. Three times a day, she swallowed one of the purple pills, and every waking hour she traced a figure-8 floating at sunset just above a smooth rock deep in Ocho Canyon.

Thanksgiving

By the time the Ochos arrived, Omaha already had over a foot of snowfall with no signs of slush. Richard picked them up on Wednesday at Eppley Airfield. Monica and Robert both agreed that the gray winter sky over Omaha was a beautiful sight they rarely saw at home.

"Wait'll you see it for five months straight," Richard returned, as he drove.

Robert was aware that this might be the only time he could talk to his brother in private; something needed to be said. "It's good that the boys are excited about this project." Richard only nodded. Robert and Monica knew that Richard still resented David for leaving his wife and son and for transporting Mexican loco weed.

From the back seat Monica said, "David is doing really well with his new job." Again Richard only nodded.

Monica rushed to break the news to Richard before they reached the house. "David would not have returned home, if Gina was there," she said. Richard drove with his eyes on the road, fearing what he knew was coming.

Robert said, "David wants Victor to move back to El Centro."

"When?" Richard asked calmly.

"Next summer."

Richard nodded.

"Will you tell Lola for us?" Monica asked the quiet

driver. Another nod. There was nothing more to be said about it.

The harvest was something Richard had always feared. He had always known that Ramone would involve Victor in the dream, with Gina and Maria to follow.

This was David's harvest. He had blown his chance for good to live at Ocho Canyon when he left Gina in Las Vegas. Fifteen years ago David had been unwilling to wait at Ocho Canyon for two decades for the harvest to arrive. In prison David Carillo had been forced to become a patient man. The weekly check he gave Gina was the best investment he could make; it gave him access to the family he had spurned.

Richard drove in glum silence the rest of the way home. Victor was his son in every sense but one, and now he and Lola would have to let him go. It would be hard on his wife, though he had warned her that the day would come when David wanted both of his sons back. Gina knew it, too. She had hoped that moving to Omaha would somehow keep Ramone away from David, if he returned to the family, or at least delay the reunion of father and son.

And now Gina Carillo had taken responsibility for her infirmity. She now blamed herself for leaping on David's car hood that long ago night, and she had not forgiven herself for putting Ramone through it all. She would speak of it in her session, so David could see it when the film was completed. Victor was set to record the cleansing confrontation from behind his camera lens early on Thanksgiving Day.

After the grueling documentary session with Gina and Robert, the entire family was silent. As the 27-pound Thanksgiving turkey turned golden in the oven, Lola and Richard were beside themselves. They had all watched

Victor film the session in Gina's bedroom. Victor had not believed what he was filming. Later, he would compare it to the film *The Exorcist,* where the devil in bedridden Gina spat black bile onto his lens and cackled at her family's horrorstruck faces, spewing insults at everyone.

For over an hour, Robert's formula brought up endless toxins accumulated during fifteen years of medications and self abuse. Robert had warned Monica before starting the session, "She's primed for a good one."

The session leaders grew exhausted from pinning Gina's strong upper body to her elevated bed to keep her from throwing herself to the floor. Poor Maria cleaned up the messes during the documentary, once begging her uncle to stop torturing her aunt. Robert never considered stopping. The blood pressure cuff around Gina's arm that Monica monitored gave her the authority to stop the session.

The most heart-rending scene came near the end, when Robert had Gina trace her purple 8 above her heart. That's when she begged for her son's forgiveness for pouring her pain into his life and causing him to be so unhappy. Ramone rushed to embrace her, and both mother and son wept for the anguish they had endured.

It was the best Thanksgiving dinner they had ever had. Gina ate a little bit of everything, savoring each bite after fasting in preparation for the session. The cranberry sauce baked into the dressing with brown sugar was Lola's specialty. The boys ate three helpings of mashed potatoes with turkey gravy.

Richard talked about Jupiter North and how much more he liked it compared to El Centro. Maria asked if she could work part-time on weekends at the concession stand. Richard said he would train her to work behind the ticket window, because they needed cashiers on weekends. Maria was happy because she wanted to make some money to buy new clothes.

Victor and Ramone said they could continue working weekends—Victor in the projection room and Ramone doing cleanup. It was apparent to the visitors that the boys wanted to stay connected to the theater in order to learn more about the film business.

Richard felt relieved, because he wanted the boys to finish high school in Omaha. Ramone had the family's attention when he told them he wanted to learn as much as he could about marketing, and that he wanted the release of *Purple 8* to be perfectly timed with the harvest.

"You have about five years," Robert told Ramone. "If you don't market it...I don't know who will."

"I'll help!" Victor declared, which Lola and Richard found a bit disturbing. Gina, who was glowing after her session, was impressed with Ramone when he asked Robert about his patent and the FDA.

"It can be marketed from Ocho Canyon, or anywhere on the reservation, until I do some more lab testing. I plan to do that next year," Robert said.

"Is it ready to be mass-marketed?" Ramone asked.

"Some states have restrictions, but California alone could use up the entire harvest, if it really took off."

"Won't the documentary help?" Victor asked.

"Of course. I think you'll have to get it on California cable stations."

Maria jumped in and asked Robert, "Could someone be injured by taking Purple 8 and then sue you?"

"That's a good question. We'd have to have disclaimers and warnings on the labels."

"Someone will sue us for sure," Victor stated. "You know how people are. They'll blame the product for their own ignorance."

"Yes, that's true, Victor," Robert returned. "That's why we'll have to pay for an airtight insurance policy. It'll cost a small fortune, but we'll make it all back when Purple 8 lives up to its advertising."

"Couldn't you treat a bunch of people at once, so you could monitor them yourself?" Ramone asked.

"Yes. With Monica's help, I've done twenty, or so."

"Why not do that each time and charge a fee that would be cheaper for each person?" Ramone suggested.

"It's possible," Monica said.

"And safer," Gina added. "I can't imagine how you could sell your formula over the counter and expect people to use it without problems. It's too radical without supervision. Victor's right...you'd be sued by every ignorant jackass out there."

"I'm working on a way to eliminate the radical stuff. I believe I can come up with a product without side effects, or fasting. I'm getting closer," Robert smiled.

On and on the family discussed Purple 8. Lola and Richard were content to have the family together in their home. Other versions of Purple 8 had supported the Carillo family sporadically. Some years better than others. Not for him. Richard was content with a steady paycheck, with no worries about a novelty product rich only in Native tradition...so far.

Saturday, Richard drove his brother around Omaha accompanied by the boys; they were looking for the right place to film the introduction at the beginning of their documentary. They found a small city park with a vacant screened-in area that had a large fire-pit, the embers of a fire still glowing orange, taking the edge off the cold November air.

Victor improvised by stepping backwards and filming as Robert spoke into the camera and moved at a slow walk. The young filmmaker said that motion would give the documentary energy for a product that increases energy.

Robert introduced himself to the camera and spoke of his family history. He related the legend of the blue cactus that had been used by his people for thousands of years. In motion, Robert mentioned all the ingredients in his formula and how the Purple 8 juice attacked deleterious parasites and released toxins stored deep in muscle tissue, explaining that these were toxins that otherwise were not flushed out of the body.

Ramone followed Victor, out of the camera's view. He was certain that his uncle's group sessions were the way to go. When Robert finished describing one of his sessions and began telling the camera about Gina's treatment, Ramone asked his uncle to do a segment promoting two-hour group sessions, describing every detail he could think of.

Robert needed no rehearsing when it came to talking about Purple 8. Robert covered every aspect, from rejuvenated red and white blood cells to improved skin tone.

Later that day Victor shot the final scene of *Purple 8*. Gina was back on camera less than 48 hours after her session. The "before and after" revealed an incredible transformation. It looked as if a plastic surgeon had worked on her face, now without the sagging skin that had given her such a discontented droopy appearance.

Victor filmed her in motion behind the walker on the sidewalk in front of their house. On camera Robert asked her how she was feeling.

"Great!"

"Any cravings for the pain killers you were taking?"

"No...no...not at all. I feel pretty good." She laughed.

By the time the Ochos returned home, Ramone was feeling disenchanted with his plan to market Purple 8. The group sessions now seemed too difficult to sell, and didn't appear to have the mass-market appeal that could fulfill his dream.

So Ramone began swirling the word "patience" inside his purple 8. The time he had left in high school really bothered him. In 2005, he would graduate. Until then, he planned to work as much as he could at the theater to pick up information about marketing the documentary. Victor had told him that *Purple 8* would run approximately forty minutes after editing.

"Something is missing," Victor had said.

"What?" Ramone asked.

Victor replied, "I don't know yet."

A Good Sign

After two years Gina had received ninety thousand dollars from David. She saved most of it. With the final thousand-dollar money order, David wrote his ex-wife a letter explaining that it would be the last payment. He wrote that he quit his job in El Centro because he was burnt out selling cars, and he hoped that the money had made up for abandoning her while she was raising their son. He went on to explain that the amount that he'd sent broke down to about five hundred dollars a month over 15 years and that he felt obligated to pay the money after being an absent father.

Now, with money in the bank, Gina could walk without her walker and was off all medication. She was grateful for David's generous back payments of child support, especially since no one had forced him to do it.

Richard and Lola had convinced David not to pull Victor out of school in Omaha before he graduated. David agreed to put the welfare of his son above his own.

Ramone and Victor spent two more summers at Ocho Canyon, and at one time were both planning to move there when they graduated. Ramone would go in five months; Victor would follow the next year. Their documentary was finished and looked fantastic to Robert and Monica, who made copies and showed it to clients, who viewed it on the reservation.

Maria did not go back to Ocho Canyon; she now had a boyfriend named Jim, a tall Anglo boy, a year older, whom she met at school. She wasn't in love with Jim—he was shy and safe. It was easy for Maria to keep her relationship with Jim platonic, because she had grown up with two women who had experienced the difficulties of being very young mothers. Maria wasn't about to give up her independence and devote herself to a child as her mother had done.

Jim was an honor student with a sweet disposition. His father was a minister and that was why Jim had such humility. He wasn't very good-looking, until you got to know what a beautiful person he was. When Jim and Maria were together in public, other people would wonder what she was doing with him.

Gina had decided to move to Phoenix when Ramone moved back to El Centro. Then Ramone surprised his mother and announced he would also move to Phoenix, if he could get his own place. Gina said she would pay his tuition and living expenses if he wanted to go to Arizona State University in Tempe. But Ramone had no interest in college. Neither did Victor. Only Maria was interested in more education after high school.

Ramone was frustrated because he hadn't come up with a solid marketing plan for Purple 8 group sessions. Brainstorming, he came up with ideas, then dismissed them after considerable thought while tracing. Ramone envied Victor, who was getting better with a camera and learning new things every day about his craft. Ramone's occupation was less glamorous; he plowed through telemarketing, mail-order and newspapers ads, and studied slick web sites. Nothing. Not one form of advertising fit his budget: pay as you go.

One spring Saturday, Maria was walking with

Ramone to work at Jupiter North when they passed an insurance company's billboard. It caught Ramone's eye and he thought it would work well to have billboards scattered on I-8 going west across Arizona. "You're right, travelers might stop to get Uncle Robert's formula," Maria said.

"Yeah. But where would they stop? Ocho Canyon is too hard to find," Ramone commented.

"Blake would be a perfect location. It's right off the interstate and it's on reservation land...so it would be legal to sell Purple 8." Maria sounded excited.

The more he thought about Blake the more Ramone was inspired. "Ya know, Maria, that might work. We could sell the documentary there, or people could view it there and talk to Robert. Robert could find out who the serious people were and start them tracing. We could come up with some sort of disclaimer that was legal, and they would have to sign it before they had a session."

When the two arrived at Jupiter North, Victor was in the projection room during a movie run. Ramone told him about Maria's idea. He asked, "Do you see anything about it that wouldn't work?" Victor thought about it for a while, then said, "I like the sound of it. It's simple and straight forward. Thousands of people use I-8 every day."

"The only way I see it working is if Uncle Robert could get clients to prepay and schedule a session. They'd have to send in the signed waiver, or bring it with them," Ramone explained.

"Lock 'em in."

"Sure, but I don't know what to put on the billboard. It would have to be something so good people would stop at Blake. Maybe I should try to get a job at a sign company in Phoenix when I move there with Mom. I could find out from the experts what works."

"Yeah...that would be good. I keep seeing all those

billboards on I-40 in New Mexico and Arizona, the ones the Navajo Nation uses to advertise their pottery, and rugs and jewelry. And, Mone, if you worked for a sign company you'd know a good deal on billboards, for sure."

"I'll call Uncle Robert and find out what he thinks. Maria is right, Blake is a perfect location."

"A toll-free number would be good, too," Victor suggested.

Ramone frowned. "Still, Uncle Robert has to screen out the abusers."

"Yeah. But somehow he knows just by looking into a person's eyes whether he's serious enough about changing his life to fast and trace," Victor said. "Don't worry about it."

Later, when Ramone called his uncle, Robert was excited about the plan. He'd never considered using Blake for his sessions.

"I guess my brother is going to have to move," he said.

First Move

Stark was about to move away from his home in Carbonville for the first time in his young life. Stark's father was a coal miner who lost his left arm in an accident unrelated to mining. Leroy Starkweather had been on his honeymoon, making a left turn with his left arm hanging outside the car window, when he was hit broadside by a drunk driver. 'Lefty' had been his nickname before his arm hit the pavement without him. Since the accident only a few buddies from the mines still called him Lefty.

Warren E. Starkweather, the young writer, preferred his nickname, Stark, because Warren was no name for a 20-year-old man raised by Lefty Starkweather, the hero of Carbonville.

Pederson Coal Company suffered a mine shaft disaster in 1979, when five coal miners lost their lives. It could've been worse, much worse, if not for Lefty Starkweather. Lefty had saved twenty-two men from certain death when he crawled and dug his way to his trapped coworkers, freeing nearly all before the shaft fell in and killed the remaining five.

The company honored Lefty's pension after his honeymoon accident and gave him full retirement. Lefty refused to take the desk job they offered him because he was not suited for pushing papers. He could barely read or write. Stark wanted to be something his old man could never be—a writer.

Stark was a high school graduate with no desire to go to college. He just kept writing without formal training. Long ago, he had run out of funny things to write about, so he wrote about the things he'd seen around the countryside in Southern Illinois. He wrote about places with no characters. He wrote about places that were stark...like himself. For hours at a time, in secluded places around Carbonville, he would sit and observe and write in his notebook the things he experienced.

The weather is bleak in early winter. Gray sky with golden hills covered with dead grass, empty gullies, and skinny leafless trees in lifeless stands with black birds flying low here and there. There is nothing but all those things...and me.

If I turn around I would see a farm, perhaps a mile away. I wonder who would live in such a lonely place. I imagine an old farmer who lives alone. He eats the same food day after day, using the same silverware, the same plate and glass for every meal.

I am in this farmer's world now, seeing what he sees every day when he looks up at this place where I now sit. This place I will call "Bleak Hill in Winter." I'll bet I'm the only person in the world who ever sat on this very spot and wrote about it. This place means nothing to me; it's just a place. There is another kind of place.

There are places in a family we can inherit, and our places stay with us for a lifetime. No matter where we go, we somehow are unable to shake that sense of position. Most of us will hold onto our invisible place as if it defined who we are.

Sometimes only an outsider can see the place you've been given. Even more rare is someone who was given an awful place when young, yet managed to escape.

My right eye is brown like my mother's eyes. It sees beauty in this place—everything is perfect just the way it is.

My left eye is blue like my father's eyes. This eye sees the farm behind me as something to be labeled and judged, made bad by a man who chose to live alone...for a loner's reasons: alcohol, shattered dreams, just plain meanness.

I close these two eyes that are not the same color. I take a deep breath and I can smell hay, not in the field, but far off and stored in the farmer's barn. It's not a stifling kind of smell, the way it can be in the summertime here, when every breath feels as if it was taken balled up inside a lawn mower's bag, the humid aroma of cut grass mixed with the haunting feeling that I will die this time of year.

I try to feel which eye is dominant, to determine if there is a pull to the way I ought to see this place. I wait and I wait while I breathe cold, clean air into my nostrils, so cold my eyes threaten to tear. But always, only one eye will tear, the brown one, my mother's eye. She has cried often, living with a man who punishes her with his self-loathing and ignorance.

I'm moving to anywhere but here. I could never become a good writer living near my father, because the words I would write would always be filled with spite, distorted by his bitter ways of seeing things. Mom cried when I told her I was leaving tomorrow. I told her I had to live my own life away from him, or I would turn out like him—mean to strangers and afraid of everything good in the world. She knew it was true.

That's why I came out here, where I've never been before, to feel what it's like to be alone in a new place.

I wanted to tell my mother more today, but she knew it all. No matter what I did here I would always be the only child of the hero of Carbonville. Mother, I used to be proud of it; I used to see it as a good thing to be known as Lefty's son. Until I watched you cry so many times.

I have to get away, Mother. I want to fall in love, and have a chance to create my own identity, away from Carbonville, in a new place where I am not just Lefty's son. I've never had a real girlfriend. I was too ashamed of that bitter old man.

When I was a little boy you would hold a mirror to my face and tell me a thousand times how rare and special I was to be given one blue eye and one brown eye. It worked; I felt no shame when the kids teased me about being a freak. You did that, Mother, for me; you gave me confidence they could not take from me. Mom, let me go while I have that confidence, and one day I will come back to you and show you I

am a writer. I must do this...for
me and for you.

Stark had saved twenty-two hundred dollars during two years canvassing door-to-door to businesses for a Carbonville chiropractor. He left his mother crying as he drove away with all his clothes and belongings jammed inside his 1980 Olds Cutlass. Lefty had grunted goodbye at the kitchen table, waiting impatiently for his breakfast and the morning paper his wife read to him every morning.

Stark had no clue where he was going. He promised his mother he'd call her when he landed somewhere. He went south, toward warm weather. He thought he'd go see Shiloh, where the famous Civil War battle took place. His great-grandpa, Warren Ellis Starkweather, had been killed there during the second day of the battle. He wanted to walk the land where it happened, and find his namesake's tombstone, if he could. It was a pilgrimage he'd wanted to make ever since he researched his great-grandfather's life at the Carbonville Public Library.

Shiloh

Stark took his time to Shiloh, spending hours writing in little out-of-the-way cafés in Illinois, Kentucky and Tennessee. Cairo, Illinois, was where his grandpa's Illinois regiment had assembled and eventually marched all the way to Shiloh.

He followed a map that showed the route the Union Army took, as close as he could, trying to maintain the army's pace each day. He wanted to know what it had been like for his grandpa's mind and body, so he slept in his car several nights, roughing it as much as he could. He wondered what effect time would have had on his grandpa's 20-year-old body, for now he was the exact same age, and figured that the effects had to be tripled because of the long march.

Stark began to fill his notebook with his thoughts:

> *It's my third day on the road. I am being pulled to Shiloh. I said goodbye to my tearful mother, just as my great-grandfather must have done when he left his family in Carbonville, not knowing if they'd ever see each other again.*
>
> *I know I'm following the*

army's route, because I ask local librarians in the small towns where I stop if they know anything about the march to Shiloh. My map is fairly accurate, and the librarians always seem to know interesting things I could never have learned on my own. Like the stragglers and deserters who stole food from gardens of Tennessee farmers, and how they would raid a farm in the middle of the night, taking chickens and pigs light enough to haul off, until they could make a fire a safe distance from the people they robbed.

But my grandpa stayed with the march at a clip of 30 miles per day. I figure I'm walking about one-third of that a day in my wanderings; that's why I'll triple how I feel when I get to Shiloh, keeping in mind that he was carrying a heavy rifle, a full canteen, and a haversack crammed with rations and stuff to sustain him. And his thoughts were on the long march to an uncertain hell that I can only imagine.

Now the sun's about to set near Mifflin, Tennessee. I'm sitting on ground a few hundred feet from my car with one thing on my mind: the future. Oh, I have plenty of money for now. The money hidden in my trunk would have been like having maybe two hundred bucks back then. Plenty of money for survival, then and now.

As I sit here seeing an occasional vehicle drive by on the road where my car is parked, I know I am not worried, as he must've been. To worry about my future is a waste of energy. Today there are thousands of soldiers in the Middle East worried as my grandpa must have worried day-to-day. As for the rest, my country is a nation of worrywarts fearful of their personal economy. If those people could have been on their way to Shiloh with my grandpa and his volunteer regiment—they would not worry about such trifles.

My grandpa left a young wife and two babies in Carbonville. Even though I will be a stranger in my new home, wherever I settle, perhaps I will meet a girl there. I've analyzed the way girls react to me when my energy is low, and when it is high. The higher the better, and my energy is highest when I am quiet inside, when my mind is not chattering to me. That is the best time to write, when I am not thinking of what I am going to write. I've noticed that when I'm busy thinking, my energy goes down and I fear most everything. I'm certain that those men marching to Shiloh had to be drained of energy and full of fear, and I predict that I too will be drained when I arrive.

My diet has to be better than theirs. I'm staying away from greasy foods for the most part, however, that's difficult to do in rural Tennessee. Every day I eat fruit and vegetables. The protein I get is in the nuts and protein bars I brought with me. I had boiled grits this morning at Hillbilly Cafe in Gadsden. I'm going to continue drinking only bottled water on the road. The water the soldiers had must have been pure back then, fetched from streams and lakes that were free of pollutants we have today.

For six days and nights, I have matched their pace to Shiloh. I have not shaved or showered since leaving home. This scraggly beard matches what the soldiers must've had in the same amount of time. My body aches in many places, ones I don't remember ever bothering me before. If I tripled my fatigue I could not imagine how sore my feet would be.

The adrenaline rush those men felt upon hearing rumors that thousands of Rebels were in the area would certainly have made them forget about the long march and their sore feet.

Today, my seventh day following the army's route, I arrived at Shiloh and walked up and down row after row of white headstones in the Union cemetery. I realized I probably would not find my grandfather's marker, because most were unmarked graves.

Shiloh's natural beauty was everywhere. Stands of bare dogwoods were abundant, arboreal relatives of those that once looked down on these lovely, manicured low hills that were once covered with thousands of bloody bodies.

I decided to follow a sign that pointed to Pittsburgh Landing down by the river, so I noted the last row of graves I had walked, in case I wanted to pick up where I left off. That way, at least I could say I passed by my grandpa's resting place.

The steep walk down to the banks of the Tennessee River was propelling me toward the infamous landing I'd read about. It was here that Union troops had disembarked from boats, only to discover thousands of their own cowering on the shore beside the cliffs. The men were petrified by the sights of carnage and the stench of fear that was all pervasive. I don't believe Grandpa Starkweather was in this place of confusion and mayhem after the first day of unimaginable slaughter. I think he must have died here on that terrible second day, along with so many of his companions. If I could find his grave marker, then I would know.

I read that this is where General Grant tried to rally his troops by riding his horse from a boat to the shoreline, urging the stragglers to battle.

Back up the steep climb to the battlefield, I ran into a park official and asked him if he knew where the 16th Illinois Regiment fought. To my surprise, he knew where all the Illinois troops had been positioned and I followed his directions on sore feet. As I walked for hundreds of yards, passing along the way monuments to other northern states, I realized I was searching for something inside me that I had always lacked: a reason to be grateful.

I needed gratitude to sustain me along my life's journey. Gratitude was something I never learned as the son of Carbonville's hero, the son of a man who risked his life so others could live.

My father had lost his battle to alcoholism after losing his arm, just like many young soldiers lost limbs here at Shiloh. In his mind, he had returned home from his honeymoon as a wounded freak, to be pitied and stared at, no longer the hero who could retire with dignity.

I have always had this feeling that he regretted my birth, because he married my mother when she became pregnant with me. Without me, there would never have been a wedding, never have been a honeymoon; and

Lefty would still have his arm. My father was an ungrateful husband and father—I never saw the hero.

Then I saw it. A tall marble monument listed my great-grandfather's regiment along with many others. I ran my fingers over his regiment's engraving and thanked my grandpa for allowing me to live today. My gratitude is all I need to take from this place. With gratitude in my heart, from this moment on, I will be transformed. I will be filled with such new energy, it will flow from me the way heat flows from a fire—and she will know right away.

Color of Kings

That early summer, Victor rode along in the U-Haul truck with Ramone and Gina, helping them on their move to Phoenix. Aunt Gina said she'd pay for his flight or bus ride home. Victor was afraid of flying, so he planned to take the bus back to Omaha.

About every hundred miles, Gina had to walk around for a half-hour to exercise her legs. Victor filmed her strolling with Ramone at rest areas. To the boys, it was truly a miracle how well Gina walked after her Purple 8 session. They all agreed that her progress should be edited into their documentary.

Gina was becoming thin and toned, getting back the petite figure she had before the accident. And, she was tracing purple 8 more than Ramone did. The new Gina was someone the boys had never known before. Now she laughed often and robustly; it was the same laugh that David had fallen in love with when they were dating.

She told the boys that she was looking forward to beginning a new life in Phoenix and dating again. "I'm thirty-seven and I want to look twenty-seven!" Then she laughed her big Irish laugh.

Ramone was a new person. His mother's restored health had given him a chance to become the confident young man he always wanted to be. To be young and now free of his mother's infirmity was putting more laughter into his heart. His plan to gain wealth from the Carillo legacy kept him tracing and pacing with boundless energy.

Ramone and Victor told Gina about Blake and the plan for Purple 8 sessions there. She liked the idea.

Already, Victor was dreading going back to finish high school in Omaha. He asked if he could finish high school in Phoenix and live with Gina, or Ramone, but Gina told him, "No way. You will finish school in Omaha first. That's final, young man."

"Richard and Lola will miss you," Ramone reminded Victor.

"That's not fair," Victor said. "I can't argue with that."

On the long trip to Arizona, Ramone studied nearly every billboard he saw, making note of how much space was used for text and what colors caught his eye. Gina thought that all the lettering on Purple 8 billboards should be purple on a white background. She said, "If the picture of the cactus is purple on the billboards, that would be a great visual reminder of where the formula comes from. Purple is the color of kings."

In Tucumcari they stayed in a motel with two double beds. The boys each massaged one of Gina's legs after she soaked in a hot bath. Blood did not circulate well to her legs if she sat for long periods of time. Pain would come and go, yet to her that was better than constant pain numbed by medication. At least now she was walking on her own.

Mornings Gina had to sit up on the side of her bed with her feet on the floor for fifteen minutes in order to get blood flowing south. She would use that time to trace her purple 8 and meditate, so deeply sometimes, an old emotion made her cry. The boys were used to her routine

114

and quietly took their turns in the shower.

Breakfast was their own fruit and orange juice along with Gina's protein bars. Diet was a huge part of her recovery, just as Robert had said it would be.

After breakfast, Gina took a long bath, letting the hot water heat up her bones. When she opened her eyes she admired her body, yet she was looking forward to the color the Arizona sun would give her pale skin. She wished David could see her with her old figure coming back. But then, just as quickly, she let his image go as she pulled herself up and out of the hot tub with her every move focused on the present. No slips, no sudden falls from a hidden emotion that could buckle her knees and ruin her progress in ridding herself of the consequences of the terrible choice she made in Las Vegas.

Out in the vast stretch of the Southwest, with beauty in all directions, going west on I-40, Gina gave Ramone the market for Purple 8 he had been seeking. It came to her when a fleet of P.I.E. semi trucks passed their U-Haul in New Mexico.

"Truckers would be an ideal market for Purple 8," Gina commented.

"No, they're always in a big hurry. They only stop to refuel, or hit a casino," Victor said.

Gina patted her nephew's knee. "Now you listen to me. When I was a waitress, I met many truckers who complained about their aches and pains. They took drugs to stay awake and ate aspirin like candy. They all had money and they yearned for a reason to stop for something that would sustain them for their long hauls. There is a constant flow on I-8 that will never end. And they would be the best word-of-mouth advertisers for Purple 8. Believe me, they would get the word out to the people who need it."

"And there's plenty of parking around Blake," Ramone added.

Gina continued, "Nowadays a lot of their wives go with them on the road. They would be a great market."

"You really think so?" Ramone asked.

"I know so," Gina insisted.

"Truckers welcome...right on the billboard," Ramone smiled.

"In purple letters," Gina laughed.

"The color of kings! King of the road!" Victor yelled.

Valley of the Sun

Gina wanted to live in Scottsdale, a prosperous, upscale part of Phoenix about which she had heard good things. They scoured apartment complexes bordering the main business district of Scottsdale for the right location for Gina, who wanted to be within walking distance to shopping, restaurants, and other services.

They found the right apartment near McDowell Road and Scottsdale Road. Within two hours the boys were unloading the U-Haul into Gina's unfurnished one-bedroom apartment on ground level. The complex had a well-equipped exercise room, a pool, sauna and hot tub. Six hundred dollars a month included utilities, and she even got a free month of rent for signing a year lease.

The boys set up her orthopedic bed first so Gina could rest. One of the things she wanted to buy soon was a queen-size bed. "I can't wait to get rid of that hospital bed!" she said.

By the time the truck was unloaded, Gina was fast asleep. The boys worked quietly, unpacking boxes and putting things away.

Ramone and Victor slept on the living room floor in central air conditioned comfort, since Gina had no furniture except her bedroom furniture.

The next morning they all lay out by the pool, soaking up Phoenix sun that hit ninety-five degrees by 10

A.M.

Then they all walked around the area together. Gina was elated to find and shop in a health food store within two blocks of her new place. They found a bank close by where she deposited her money.

The appeal of Scottsdale made Victor want to stay for the entire summer, especially if Ramone could get a job and his own place.

That night, Gina made a healthy meal of pasta and a huge garden salad that the boys devoured like wolves.

With two days remaining on their truck rental, Victor rode along with Ramone, hunting for a sign company in the area. They stayed in the right lane in heavy traffic, going up and down Scottsdale and Tempe main streets with no luck. Then, on Apache Avenue in Tempe, Victor spotted a rundown shanty that housed a business named Tempe Signs; whereupon Ramone drove onto the dirt lot and parked in the shade of a lone palm that darkened the exterior of the one-story building.

In the hot sun, they squinted at a barking mongrel dog chained to a pole near two silver truck trailers located at the back of the lot that looked as if they were used for storage.

They entered the cool, cluttered office where a middle-aged secretary met them with friendly, sparkling brown eyes above glasses that rode the tip of her nose.

"Hi!" She greeted the young men.

"I'm looking for work," Ramone smiled.

"Well, you may just be in the right place!" She grinned at him. "I'm Mary."

She extended her hand above a messy desk covered with receipts and samples of graphic designs in colors that caught Victor's keen eyes.

"Ramone Carillo." He shook her hand. "This is my

brother, Victor."

Mary was impressed with the young men, especially dark and handsome Victor.

In a nearby office they could hear the owner, John Bullock, on the phone, chewing out someone for getting his order wrong.

"John will be off the phone soon," she smiled and offered them coffee, which they refused.

"Where are you fellas from?"

"Omaha. I just moved here with my mother," Ramone replied. "Victor is just visiting."

"You have any experience working with signage?"

"No, I just graduated from high school. Do you sell billboard advertising?"

"We sure do. We have over a hundred locations around the valley. We do all kinds of signage: vehicle lettering, magnetics, graphics, everything but neon."

When John came out of his office, Mary introduced him to the young men. The former economics professor with the big black mustache was friendly and suggested that Ramone could telemarket; his job would be finding advertising clients in the valley.

John gave Ramone and Victor a quick tour of the business, showing Ramone the desk he would use, starting the next day.

"My telemarketer is off for a couple weeks. The job pays three hundred a week, if you can do forty hours a week. You can do as many hours as you want...twenty or thirty...whatever you want."

"Forty is fine," Ramone said, as he eyed the stack of Metro Phoenix Yellow Pages beside the desk.

John showed Ramone the phone script he'd use when contacting the public. It listed all the types of signage they offered.

"That was too easy," Ramone told his brother, as they drove away from Tempe Signs. "I can't believe I start Monday, just like that."

"It's the tracing, Mone...you created it."

"Call your dad and tell him I got a job, and see if you can stay longer."

"For the summer?"

"See what he says. I'll be able to get my own place in a month, or so."

Gina was impressed that Ramone had gotten a job so quickly. On behalf of the boys, she called Lola and Richard and asked them if Victor could stay longer.

"That's fine," they said on the phone, "as long as he's back by the start of his school year."

Gina gave them her new address and phone number. Lola told Victor she'd send him more summer clothes.

Gina kept soaking up the sun, however she never stayed out for more than fifteen minutes at a time...up to three times a day. She loved her new home because its location was conducive to walking. Lots of walking. After two weeks in Phoenix she was walking three miles a day, and now weighed the same as when she first met David.

Victor often walked with Ramone to work, taking along his digital camera to film the empty Salt River, the Arizona State University campus, and rugged mountains: Camelback, South Mountain, and the distant, larger Superstitions.

"Have you heard about The Superstitions and the Lost Dutchman's Gold Mine?" Victor asked his brother.

"Don't you remember? My mom used to read about 'em to us at Blake."

"Oh, yeah, that's right. I'd love to film the other side of The Superstitions. There's supposed to be more rattlesnakes there than anywhere else in the world."

"That's why I'm not goin' with ya."

At Tempe Signs, some fifty yards behind the office, there was an ancient Airstream trailer parked under a palm tree that bordered the fenced property line. One day, Ramone decided to check it out.

Once inside the hot, stuffy trailer cluttered with cans of paint and boxes of discarded plastic letters, Ramone could see himself living there. "What do you think, Vic? It'll take a lot of work."

"I think you should go talk to The Man."

They found John in his office. "Would you rent that old trailer to me?" Ramone asked his boss.

"If you want to clean it out. It's got a window air conditioner in the bedroom. You can keep the sofa that's in there. I suppose fifty bucks a month for power. A dollar a day for water."

"Eighty bucks a month. I'll take it," Ramone said.

""I'll clean it up, Mone...while you're workin'," Victor offered.

Since Ramone started working for Tempe Signs, he had generated many good leads for Tex, their salesman, who was closing deals at a good clip. So John was happy to let Ramone live in the Airstream.

On his break, Ramone wandered back to inspect Victor's cleaning. He had everything out of the trailer and was mopping the floor. "Next, I'm gonna wipe down the walls and ceiling, and clean all the windows," Victor said.

Ramone opened all the windows in the stuffy trailer. "Not bad for eighty bucks a month, huh?" he asked.

"Are you kiddin'? This place is gonna be great! Since Gina's gettin' a new bed you can put her old bed in the back bedroom...and I'll sleep on the couch."

"I don't want her bed. I'll put a mattress on the floor."

"I gotta get a cover for this couch. I tried to pound the dust out, but there's too much. I cleaned out the fridge, but the oven's in bad shape."

"Forget the oven. I won't use it. I'll buy food I don't have to cook. It's too hot to cook anyway."

"The A/C works. I turned it on after John turned on the power. All the lights work, too. God, I can't believe you got this place for only eighty bucks a month. You'll be able to save money for your billboards."

Ramone agreed with his brother while he tried to see himself living there alone after Victor left. He couldn't visualize it now, so, he traced until he saw that this home was temporary, just until he could save enough money to rent a nicer place.

The temperature in the valley was increasing every day. Ramone and Victor lived well together despite the confining space in the Airstream.

Uncle Robert had called to say he was coming to visit them in a week. He told his nephew that his new formula used the body's natural elimination process to clean out toxins in thirty-six hours after ingestion. Robert and Monica were elated about this breakthrough, because no fasting was required, making it much easier on new consumers of Purple 8.

Monica had discovered a way to skip the fasting by reducing the amount of Purple 8 taken during the first session. The results were the same after thirty-six hours, without the drastic spewing of toxins that Robert had worried would scare off most prospects.

Robert told Ramone that Victor should film the new and improved formula's easier directions. Ramone said he would be willing to take the new formula and add it to the documentary after his mother's session. "Just so long as Victor isn't going to film me taking a dump," he joked.

Energy

Every morning in the Airstream, Ramone woke up breathing like a bulldog with congestion. The window air conditioner blowing down and across his mattress was clogging his sinuses; Victor slept comfortably on the sofa with a floor fan in the main room.

Ramone was getting tired of living in the cramped quarters. His morning shower was a drizzle from a rusty shower head that sprayed and sputtered like a broken squirt gun. He missed the morning walk to work from his mother's place; it had been his chance to breathe and wake up his body before eight hours of sedentary phone work. From a confining sardine can to his desk without breakfast, not to mention a nasal voice like Elmer Fudd, added up to be a miserable morning.

Then boisterous Tex would come into the closed telemarketing room smoking a cigarette while he drank his coffee. Since Tex was getting good leads from Ramone, he was happy to answer the questions his lead generator asked him every morning. They were questions Ramone and Victor brainstormed the night before, after spending fifteen minutes tracing. Tracing was Ramone's idea, a way to keep Purple 8 alive.

One morning, after Ramone finished his first call and blew his nose into a paper towel, a young man strolled into the office. Ramone noticed that the guy's eyes were different colors. He was dressed casually in shorts, T-shirt and sandals.

"Hey Stark! Welcome back!" Tex barked while Ramone made his next call.

"Hey Tex!"

They shook hands. Tex asked, "Stark, did everything go okay back home at your father's funeral?"

"My mom's doin' better," Stark said, meaning she was doing better after her husband died. "It's good to be back though."

John entered and welcomed his telemarketer back. After Ramone wrapped up yet another lead for Tex, John introduced Stark to Ramone. They shook hands.

"I'll use the other desk," Stark said to John.

"I'll get a phone right away and set you up," John replied and left the room with Tex.

"I could work at that desk if you want your desk back," Ramone offered.

"No, no, that's fine...I'll use this one."

It didn't take long before Ramone realized that his coworker was a pro on the phone. They began to compete in a friendly way that made the morning fly by. Between calls they would chat with their backs to each other.

"You from Phoenix, Ramone?"

"I'm from El Centro, but I moved here from Omaha."

"Never been to either place. El Centro's in California, right?"

"Yeah...between Yuma and San Diego."

"Too cold in Omaha?"

"Yeah. My mom didn't like it at all. I moved here with her."

"You live with her here?"

"She has her own place in Scottsdale. My brother

125

and I are living in John's trailer out back."

"Yeah? I bunked there for a few weeks when I first moved here. John's good about helping people out."

"Where're you from, Stark?"

"Carbonville in southern Illinois. I just got back from there. My dad died of lung cancer. He got it from working in the coal mines. Black Lung they call it."

On their lunch hour, Ramone got Victor and the three of them ate at a nearby restaurant. Victor brought along his digital camera and told them he was going to film a bit around the ASU campus to see if he could meet any girls.

"Girls love this guy," Ramone told Stark.

"You two don't look like brothers."

"We have the same father. My mother was Mexican," Victor said.

Stark was fascinated when they told him about the documentary they had made. He wanted to know all about the formula and tracing. That led to Stark telling them about his belief in body energy levels. He told them his discovery must be related to their uncle's formula.

All afternoon, between calls, Stark told Ramone how he had worked for a chiropractor back home who gave him an electrical impulse stimulator that he placed on points on his jaw and on the back of his neck where it activated endorphins and adrenaline to increase his energy.

"I know it works because of the way other people react around me. It's safe. I use it every morning. You should try it sometime," Stark suggested with animation.

Early that evening, Victor and Ramone walked over to Gina's place to have dinner as heavy traffic sliced past them in both directions.

"Did you notice that Stark has one brown eye and

one blue eye?" Victor asked.

"Yeah...so what?"

"I've seen dogs with two different colored eyes...but never a person."

"He's a writer."

"Really?" Victor was surprised.

"He said he could write a novel about Purple 8 and that the book could be marketed to truck stops long before the billboards went up. He's got some amazing ideas...and is he ever good on the phone!"

"Did he say anything else about the documentary?"

"Only that it could be a great marketing tool."

Victor mentioned, "I could create art for the book's cover."

"Stark says it has to grab truckers...men and women."

"I had this dream one night. I was flying above I-8 headed west toward Blake...and I could see a semi truck passing a billboard that had purple letters on a white background that read: Purple 8 / Last Chance / Next Exit. And the next exit was Blake. And Blake was painted purple with eight white doors and dozens of truckers parked around it. It was so cool, Mone! I could really see it!"

"I can see it, too! But can Stark write? That's the question I want answered. If he can't write...the book won't help us market the formula."

"Writing a novel and getting it published seems like a long and slow way to market Purple 8."

"It's okay...we've got four years till the harvest. When you graduate, we'll have three years to go. Time is one big illusion, brother Victor. It'll pass. Remember what Uncle Robert always tells us...."

"I know...I know...all we have is now," Victor grumbled.

"And don't worry about getting it published. If it's good...I'll publish and market the heck outta it to truck stops on the phone. Stark already knows that it will work."

"What did he say?"

"Nothin'. I can see it."

"Wasn't that wild when he talked about that energy stuff?"

"I'm gonna try that thing he puts on his jaw and use it while I'm tracing."

"I might try it, too, just to see what it does. He says that people react to him in a more positive way after he uses it. He says it's like radar for girls. He said he gets ignored by everybody when he doesn't use it."

"Maybe my mom should try it," Ramone said.

"Maybe. She looks good, doesn't she, Mone?"

"Yeah...thanks to Purple 8."

"And her positive attitude!"

"Yep...that's everything," Ramone agreed.

Stark's Place

A couple of weeks later, Stark invited the Carillo brothers to his apartment in Mesa. Stark told Ramone there was a vacancy coming up at the end of the month in his apartment complex and suggested he check out his place to see what he thought of it.

Ramone and Victor were both tired of living in the Airstream; being so close to work was burning out Ramone. Since John paid Ramone three hundred bucks every Friday, he had managed to save over seven hundred of the nine hundred he'd been paid. Stark thought Ramone could move into a studio apartment like his for $525.00 first month's rent, plus a hundred dollar deposit, so it was worth looking into.

Stark picked them up in his car and drove them over to his place, six miles away. Mesa was a clean city and growing fast, like the rest of the valley. Stark's two-story complex was older and had a pool in the courtyard. Ramone and Victor liked the idea of diving into that pool after work.

Stark's studio apartment was on the first floor. It was a spartan place with floor pillows, a 12-inch color TV on a table, and a floor mattress partitioned off by a black tri-folded divider that Stark had bought at a garage sale. The most notable things about Stark's place was its cleanliness and the stacks of books against a wall. An air purifier blew fresh oxygen from atop the yellow refrigerator.

Stark was proud of his place. He had come to Mesa alone, without knowing anybody in the area. Like Ramone, he got lucky and found John, who gave him a chance to prove himself.

He played a Neil Young CD on a portable CD player resting on the floor near the mattress. The music played low as the trio talked on and on about Purple 8 and the book Stark had begun to write. He told the brothers he'd written most of the first chapter. "I'll finish it in a few days, type it, then let you read it. But I need more facts about your uncle's formula, the history of it."

"What's the title of your book?" Victor asked.

Their host went over to his CD player and turned it off. "*Places*. There are places in a family that you inherit, places your family gives you according to your birth order, or who they want you to be. It's insane, I know, but most of us are born with this invisible place in our family."

"That's our family!" Victor declared.

"Mine too. I believe everyone comes from a place loaded with emotional baggage. I mean, if you ask a girl where she's from, she's going to say St. Louis, Chicago, or Hattiesburg. It's later on when you find out about this other place she's from. Maybe her place is the first born, or the only child who is a hard-driven achiever. Or maybe her place is to be the victim caught in the middle of her family's fire, and she fought for a better place in her family, until she gave up and played the role they gave her."

"Places," Ramone mumbled while tracing.

Victor was not tracing, he was letting his mind run away, while his body sprawled spread eagle on a floor pillow, his eyes not seeing the ceiling because the book's title held all of his attention.

"What's your place?" Ramone asked Stark.

"My place is a solitary kind of place, one I've

learned to be content with. I'm an only child. I inherited my father's anger and my mother's fear. My place was to not disturb their drama, to ignore it. That's why I write."

"To create your own place?" Victor said.

"Exactly. It's my journey to accept that place and move on to a better place."

Ramone told Stark, "It would be good if you had a session with my uncle when he comes to visit. That's how you can find out all about Purple 8."

"I'd like that. Do you guys want to try that impulse stimulator I told you about?"

Ramone answered for both of them when he told Stark that Gina thought they should check with Robert before trying anything like that.

Stark's eyes were easy for Ramone to see up close. The blue eye was on fire, shining brighter than his brown eye. He told Ramone at work that his brown eye was the color of his mother's eyes. But the blue eye was favored—because it was the blue eye of his full-blooded Cherokee father. He told Ramone how his father's people had been a fair-skinned blue-eyed band in North Carolina when Stark's great-grandparents were forced from their land by the U.S. Government.

"My father's place was to be the first Starkweather to break his family's bloodline. My dad believed his arm was taken because of it. His wedding band hadn't been on his left hand for a day when that car smashed his arm off at the elbow. Right after it happened, he jammed his elbow into his side to slow the bleeding while he searched for his arm on the street. He brought it back to the car and had my mom pull his wedding band off his finger, while he drove himself to a hospital."

"He thought he was being punished for not marrying a full-blood?" Victor asked.

"Yeah. Superstitious, huh?" Stark grinned.

"Who can blame him, for God's sake!" Ramone said.

"And on his honeymoon," Victor shook his head in disbelief.

Stark commented, "An accident like that can put you and your family in a bad place, a place that never gets better. I'm happy for my mother that he died. Maybe now she can make a better place for herself in her new life."

Later, the trio strolled the ASU campus with gregarious Victor stopping pretty coeds to ask them if they'd be in his next documentary. Ramone appeared content and not at all envious of his brother, even though the coeds were lost in Victor's charm.

Stark mused, "I have to say that I am glad to have somehow met you and Victor. I'm learning so much about myself from both of you."

First Place

By August 1st, Ramone and Victor had moved into an apartment upstairs from Stark. They considered this studio their first place. Though the Carillo brothers had no furniture and shared the same floor mattress, they never complained. Ramone's sinus problems cleared up the moment he moved out of the Airstream. Victor was aware that this was his last month in Phoenix and dreaded going back to Omaha to live with his family. He told his brother, "It's not that they are a problem to live with. They're great. It's just that it feels good to be on my own every day."

"But you're not on your own. You're on vacation. I'm payin' for this place. I don't mind you stayin' here, bro, but when you move here for good, you'll have to pay your way."

"I know, Mone. I mean...it's great to see you in your own place. It inspires me. But when I go back, you and Stark will make all these incredible things happen. I want to be here to read his chapters and discuss the story with him and be here when Purple 8 is launched. It's all so...unfair."

"Cheer up, bro. Your senior year will fly by if you trace more. That's what I did. It killed the clock time that was dragging by and showed me that time is an illusion. Tracing will keep you in the present and away from the future. See, like Uncle Robert says, 'There's only one time that's real: Now.' Victor, if you don't trace and your attention stays on your emotions...you will have a very long battle with time in your mind."

"I know. I'm not in my mind," Victor acquiesced.

"You might as well trace more now while you're here instead of thinking about how little time you have left."

"Easy for you to say. You've probably been tracing while you're talking to me, haven't you?"

Ramone smiled, knowing his brother was going to have a long winter whether or not he traced, because Omaha winters could be more confining than that Airstream.

Gina drove over in a red '89 Firebird convertible to see her son's new place. She had purchased the car yesterday from a neighbor for $2200.00. After she saw her son's barren space she told him it was time he bought himself a bed and a table.

"Come on. I've got a charge card at Goldwaters and you can make the payments. You can't live like this, Ramone."

Ramone drove the Firebird with the top down even though the temperature outdoors was 107 degrees. He said, "Mom, could you help me get a car? My friend Stark takes me to work and back. I can't even visit you when I want to. It's too far to walk, now."

Gina grinned at her son. "Funny thing," she said. "I bought this car for you. I don't need a car. My spa and all my shopping is within walking distance. So happy birthday and merry Christmas for about the next ten years!" She laughed gaily.

From the middle of the back seat Victor knew now that he could not return to Omaha. Since Ramone had a car, life would be independent and ripe with all kinds of possibilities, versus nine months up north in that freezer where the winter blues were real and too powerful for him to overcome by tracing.

Then Gina asked Ramone about the plot of Stark's book, Places.

"I'm not really sure what it's about. He told us that the title refers to the places you can inherit in a family. I don't know much more than that."

Gina told Ramone, "I expect to see you often now that you have wheels."

"I will, Mom."

"It's not free you know. You have to get liability insurance on it tomorrow."

"No problem, Mom." Ramone smiled.

Later that night, after dinner at Gina's, the boys picked up Stark and drove over to downtown Tempe with the top down. They went to a coffee house where local musicians played live music.

Stark teased an attractive counter girl. He told her while he kept his eyes closed, "If you can guess what color my eyes are, I'll double your tip."

She guessed blue and he'd open his brown eye. Then he gave her another chance, and she said brown, so he opened his blue eye. He was really funny.

Earlier, when Ramone dropped off Gina after picking out his furniture, the boys had walked her to her apartment. Ramone had just lifted her 5-gallon water jug onto the dispenser, when Maria called from Omaha. She was flying to Phoenix that weekend to spend the last two weeks of summer break with the boys.

"There goes my bed," Ramone droned to Victor.

Victor replied, "You know, she's coming here to

make sure I come back."

"Maybe that's a part of it, who knows. I can't blame her for wanting to come here."

The next day after work, Ramone borrowed John's truck so he and Victor could pick up the new bed and dinette set and save the thirty-dollar delivery charge. On his lunch break, he bought insurance for his car, so Gina could sign the title over to him.

Meanwhile Stark kept writing Places. When he heard that Maria was coming to visit—he used it in his story. He wrote in longhand for four hours; typed, it would come out to twelve pages. Before finally falling asleep, he had made Maria the love interest in his story, and traced like Ramone had taught him to do.

When Light Comes

Stark waited on the back seat of the parked convertible. The trunk was open and waiting for Maria's luggage at the airport. There she was, walking between the boys; she was beautiful and seventeen, just like his character Marie in his novel. The real girl was about 5'3" in her sandals, her black hair thick and full—details he intended to give to the love interest in his story.

He kept his dark shades on so he could stare at the most beautiful girl he'd ever laid eyes on. She was wearing shades, too. Her skin was dark like Victor's. She wore frayed cut-off denim shorts with a black t-shirt. Unobtrusive silver jewelry circled her wrists and fingers, along with a thin silver necklace supporting a crucifix.

Her red lipstick made her teeth look whiter than salt and enhanced her small oval mouth. She smiled at him when she slid onto the back seat. Her sweet perfume entranced him.

"Hi, Stark. I'm Maria."

When he took her hand, he wanted to see her eyes behind her dark lenses, so he removed his glasses and let her see his eyes. His tracing had helped him be that direct. He felt pleased when she removed her glasses as well.

When Ramone got behind the wheel after stowing Maria's luggage, Victor hopped onto the front passenger seat and turned to face the two in back.

Stark felt that the boys were wary of him now. They were listening to every word he spoke to Maria.

"Where are you from, Stark?" she asked.

"Carbonville...in Illinois."

After a while, Maria announced, "I broke up with my boyfriend. But I'm not too upset about it; he was becoming too demanding with his religious, conservative ideas."

"You like Omaha?" Stark asked her.

"Oh, it's alright...sometimes."

"Well, alright then," he replied.

She laughed. He liked her laugh.

"You're seventeen...right?"

She nodded yes.

During their short conversation, Stark had been mentally revising what he wrote the night before. His imagination had fallen short of the truth. The young girl he had added to his story needed to be smarter and full of life, full of energy.

"I wrote a lot last night," he said.

"Really?" Ramone replied as he drove them toward Tempe.

"It's nice here, Mone," Maria said, looking at the scenery.

"Hey, we should hike the Superstitions tomorrow!" Victor exclaimed. "Show Maria some real mountains."

"Yeah, a hike sounds good," Maria returned.

They stopped at Gina's place in Scottsdale. Maria could hardly believe how good her aunt looked and how well she was getting around without any pain.

Gina invited Maria to stay with her, but Ramone told his mother that he was giving up his bed for Maria and that they were hiking the Superstitions the next day.

"The Superstitions? Good God, Ramone, that place is a wasteland in the summer! There's snakes and heat—you could die from thirst out there."

"We'll take water, Aunt Gina," Victor hugged his aunt. "Stark knows a good trail."

"We gotta start very early...when light comes," Stark said.

"I'm gonna take my video camera. Whatever I shoot, I want to send to Mom and Dad."

"Send it? Why don't you just show it to them when you get back?" Gina asked.

"I'm not going back." Victor sounded belligerent.

Everyone stared at Victor, until Maria said, "Dad wants you to graduate in Omaha with me."

"I don't care what he wants! I can go to school here and not deal with another awful winter. My blood doesn't like that climate. I want to live here with Ramone. Dad can't make me go back."

Gina asked Victor to sit down with her at the kitchen table. Ramone and Maria also took chairs. Victor stubbornly crossed his arms in front of his chest, while Ramone traced, listening to his mother's soft words.

"Victor, if I thought you would pull this kind of stunt, I would never have moved here. I know how important it is to your parents to have you graduate with Maria. They've been saving for your college...I'm sure you could go to ASU...if you want to."

"I don't want to go to college. They can keep that money, Aunt Gina. If they say I can't go to high school here...then I'll go back to El Centro and live with my real dad. I'd rather go to school there than Omaha."

"Your *real* dad? Your *real* dad is Richard, the man who raised you and was there for you when your *biological* dad was in prison and in Mexico doing God knows what!"

"Robert might not let us use Blake to sell Purple 8, if you don't graduate in Omaha," Ramone said.

Gina added, "Look Victor, I'll make you a deal. If you finish school there, I'll pay your way out here for Christmas break. Then you'll only have a few months to go."

"Mom and Dad would be devastated, Victor, if you didn't graduate with me!" Maria cried.

Just when Victor was being hammered on all sides, Stark surprised everyone when he spoke up from the sofa. "Victor, you must graduate in Omaha."

They all looked at Stark and waited for his reasons. Stark stood and walked toward them without looking at anyone; he was selecting his words as he circled the table with all eyes on him.

"Victor, the way I see it...it's your place to do this very last thing that your parents want you to do. If you don't...you'll wander in circles and die out here without support. You are not the kind of guy to quit on the place in the family they have given you. And it's not Ramone's place to be your guardian. Your adoptive parents have been good to you. They'll resent Ramone for your decision. Honor them and get your diploma in Omaha...and then make your own place."

Victor had been swayed by the time Stark sat back down on the sofa.

"Well, it would be nice to visit here at Christmas when it's so frigin' cold there," Victor smiled.

Maria smiled at Stark; she was thankful he had changed her brother's mind.

Gina was impressed with Stark's maturity and his words about Victor's place in the family. She was clear about Richard's place in the Carillo family. Richard was the youngest brother and had dropped out of high school in the tenth grade so he could help support his elderly mother.

Richard developed a passion to return to high school, when he was turned down for good city jobs he applied for. Finally, after going to night school, Richard passed a high school equivalency exam. Then he got the job at The Jupiter. Gina could now see that Richard had assigned places to Maria and Victor—his children were to be educated and never dismissed when the good jobs required a diploma.

Certainly, Gina knew about these places in a family, places that become a part of you and can never be shaken. She thought of the place she had been given, a place she had not escaped. It was a place she tried to keep when she married David, a place that made her a one-man woman, just like her mother had been.

A Walk in the Shade

To the east of Apache Junction, on a gravel road Stark knew, they all watched for a trail that would lead them into the Superstitions. Ramone drove his car slowly, evading deep rain ruts as best he could.

Maria was on the front passenger seat applying sunscreen to her exposed skin, when Stark pointed out the trail he had found last winter when he came to the mountains alone to write about his dying father.

They each carried a plastic bottle of frozen water that Stark gave them when he knocked on Ramone's door at 4:30 that morning, just over an hour ago. No breakfast. Stark insisted they eat after their hike, and gave them each a protein bar that he said would tide them over.

Last night, Stark had written for two hours after he left Ramone's apartment. Maria was having fun on her vacation, but not with him. When Ramone noticed Stark staring at Maria in her bathing suit, he had told his gawking friend that she was too young for him.

"I'm twenty-one, and she's almost eighteen. Besides that," Stark replied, "you don't know where we've been."

"What do you mean?"

"Age has nothing to do with people. It's who they are inside, and how they help each other to reach their full potential. I know she's a beautiful person inside, that's obvious. You don't have to worry about me. Besides, it's always up to the girl what happens."

A few minutes later, Maria had come in with Victor after their late night swim. She had a beach towel wrapped around her when she sat on the floor between Ramone and Stark, and asked Stark how he first knew that he wanted to be a writer.

"I used to go out in the the country and write. I always felt better after writing, though most of what I wrote I'd throw away."

"Why?" Maria asked.

"Wasn't any good. It's not what you write...it's what you keep."

After an awkward pause he told Maria he'd like to write about her, a character like her.

"Why me?" she inquired.

"My leading character falls in love with this beautiful girl, and you're the only beautiful girl I know."

Maria was flattered.

"Don't worry, I won't use your real name, or embarrass you. Her name is Marie in the story. Just be yourself and Marie will come to life."

"What's the story about?"

"I don't know exactly. I have to find out more about Purple 8 from your uncle when he comes. It would be about that."

"Uncle Robert's coming to Phoenix?" she asked Ramone.

"In a week."

"Good, I'll get to see him."

Now they followed a narrow trail and eventually crossed paths with an older couple carrying yellow backpacks. Stark asked them if the trail was a good one for seeing the Superstitions. They replied that it was the only way in that wasn't too strenuous.

The sun was rising orange-hot before them. Victor led the way with Maria and Ramone just behind him. They all wore shades and baseball caps to shield their eyes from the sun. Stark often lagged behind so he could scribble down things in his notebook:

> *...faded green cactus in all directions; jackrabbits with powerful legs ran kicking wild until vanished in sagebrush; Superstitions change colors with rising sun, from a gray purple to black and brown with ominous boulders bigger than houses; sun is oppressive, as if sticking your head in a hot oven with your hat on; I could smell Maria's sweet perfume when coming close to her on the trail; it feels so good to be around a beautiful girl who doesn't belong to anyone but herself.*

Ramone was wary of snakes. So, he traced, believing that if he washed himself in purple the snakes would know and stay away.

Maria talked about her ex-boyfriend with Victor, because her brother knew him from school. She explained that she grew tired of going to his church with him and his parents, then afterwards going to brunch with them to the same restaurant, where the same church crowd went every Sunday. She said, "Jim complained about the clothes I wore; and if I wore lipstick, he always made some negative comment about how I was trying to copy skinny models in fashion magazines and how phony that was."

"Why did you like that guy?" Stark asked from behind her.

"What?" she asked, turning back to him.

"You must have liked some things about him. He was your boyfriend, right?"

"He was smart," she laughed. "And at first I felt very comfortable around him."

Stark held back from grilling her, for he had never been one of the brainy guys in Carbonville High, and he didn't think any girl would feel comfortable around him, until he did himself.

"Hey, Ramone, how's your billboard coming for Purple 8?" Maria asked.

"I'm learning a lot about design and location. I think the key is if Stark can write a good book that promotes Purple 8...readers will notice the billboard and be our best prospects."

"Otherwise...they'll just drive by," Victor said.

"The new formula has no side effects, no fasting, either," Ramone told Maria.

Just then, Ramone saw a huge rattlesnake coiled about ten yards off the trail to their right and pointed at it. "Look at the snake!" He stopped to gape.

Stark told them to keep going. "Snakes don't want any trouble, but don't step on one," he advised.

It was too far to hike into the heart of the Superstitions with their scanty water supply. By the time they reached the sloping, rugged mesa it was getting too hot to go on. Victor had dropped his water bottle and lost most of it to the thirsty desert. They all shared with him, and Stark thought it best they head back.

"We're not even close to seeing what's on the other

side!" Victor complained.

"We're not camels. Our water's low," Stark said.

They headed back, inspired by the downhill track and the fact that they were hungry. Stark led the way this time. Though they hadn't gone as far into the Superstitions as they wanted, they had a respect for the savage beauty the Apaches knew. Stark realized that he was with three Native Americans who loved this part of the country.

He wrote later:

> *Victor walked tall without effort, his lean body moving fluidly without fatigue after miles on this baked and rutted earth. Ramone had it too, this remarkable ability to not show fatigue with hardly any sweating. And Maria was the most remarkable. Though she appeared feminine, without physical athletic definition...she moved gracefully on powerful legs that gained strength with distance. As with her brother and cousin, there was no sense of wear about her; it was as if she were going for a walk in the shade with no concern for time or thirst.*

"Did I tell you I'll be taking a drama class this year?" she asked the boys.

"You still want to be an actress?" Ramone scoffed playfully.

146

"I want to see if I'm good at it. If I am, I'll take a class in college."

"You have the looks for it," Stark said from the point.

"I'm not naive about it. I know it's hard work and not as easy as it looks. Good actors make it look easy, because they learn to relax on stage and in front of the camera."

"That's true for about everything," Stark said. "Relaxation is success, I believe."

"Did you move here alone, Stark?"

"Uh huh."

"That's brave."

"Not really. I was running away from home."

"Carbonville?"

"Yeah. You know, I just thought of something. When I first left home, I went to Shiloh where the Civil War battle took place. I wanted to trace the march my great-grandpa took. He died there."

"He was from Carbonville?" Maria asked.

"Yeah. I felt brave at first when I left home...like he must have. Then at Shiloh I got scared. At the time I thought I was scared because I was in the very place where those men faced death. But now I know I was scared for me and where I was going...and what I would do to survive in this crazy world. I don't believe I need a college degree to survive...I know that survival is a long way from prosperity. And I don't mean just money, either. Since I've moved here, I've prospered. I have my own place and, now, I look forward to every new day more than I ever did back home. To me...that's prosperity."

"That's beautiful, Stark. I'd really like to read your book," Maria said.

"It's too early. I'm glad you're here, though. I

mean...bein' around guys all the time is not good for balance. If you know what I mean."

"I think so."

They drank two pitchers of iced tea when they had lunch at an Apache Junction café after their hike. During their meal, Ramone told Stark about Gina's accident in Las Vegas and described their lives at Blake while David was in prison. Stark was fascinated with the Carillo family's turbulence mixed in with the legacy and Ocho Canyon.

Maria watched Stark's eyes across the table as he listened to their family history. She could see that each of his mismatched eyes had a kind of separateness to them. His brown right eye was brighter than his blue eye; and the blue eye appeared cold and distant compared to the brown one that seemed lit with compassion and more life.

Victor noticed his sister's interest in Stark, but then he dismissed it, because he thought that she liked him because he and Ramone liked him.

My Father's Eye

Stark joined them for a vegetarian dinner at Gina's apartment that night. He was moved by Gina's words about her recovery since having a Purple 8 session. Then he watched the documentary. He asked Gina a thousand questions about her life, which made him a welcome guest. Gina poured out the details of her past, admitting that she chose to suffer during most of it.

Ramone traced most of the evening, knowing he, too, had come a long way since those awful days at Blake.

Chatting in Gina's living room after dinner, Stark asked if any of them were up for a walk. Only Maria said yes. Victor held back, because he wanted to talk to his parents. Gina had mentioned that she planned to call them and tell them she was paying for Victor and Maria's bus fare home. Gina was most anxious to hear what Victor had to say to Richard and Lola.

The night air had cooled to 92 degrees as Stark and Maria strolled along the Scottsdale sidewalk. They were walking toward a residential area, where single-family homes built in the '70s seemed to never end. Maria matched her companion's quick pace while recounting more about Gina's amazing life.

"I remember Gina reading to all of us from her bed at Blake. She was like this really strict teacher. I never had a teacher as tough as Gina. Not tough in a bad way. She was so insistent that we read diverse things, from classics to the newspaper. And she wouldn't allow us to speak Spanish. Even my mother was her pupil. Gina demanded that Mom learn to speak and read English. Sometimes Gina would drink vodka mixed with o.j. when she felt bad. Then she would yell at us if we goofed off. She was so crazy," Maria laughed.

"Enough about Gina. I want to know more about Maria."

"What do you want to know?"

"Your dreams. The things you want for yourself," he said.

"Well...I'd like to be healthy, and happy, with work I love, and no money problems. I saw enough of that in El Centro and I know I want no part of that."

"So you go to college for four years, and pick a profession that pays big bucks so you can buy lots of things."

Maria frowned. "You make it sound bad. What's up with that?"

"I guess I'm just one of the average guys who survive without college. There's plenty of us. Ramone won't need college. He'll get Ocho Canyon when he gets married. I guess his dad really blew it when he divorced Gina."

"She divorced him. Besides, David couldn't live there because he didn't want to."

"But since Robert has no son, Ramone gets it when he marries."

"That's right."

"Isn't David the oldest son?"

"Yes."

"So Ramone's first in line. What if David remarries?"

150

"Doesn't matter. It's always the eldest son in every new generation that inherits the legacy."

"It's a crazy thing, isn't it?" Stark said.

"Not really. It keeps new blood living there."

"So, if Robert had been the first brother to have a son, then he could keep living there until his son married?"

"He could live there until he died, if his son wanted him to live there with his family."

"So when Ramone marries...it's his?"

"If he wants it."

"Why wouldn't he want it?"

"I don't know. He has to want to live there full-time...and Monica and Robert have to want to leave."

"How do you feel about it?" Stark asked.

"What?"

"This male-only legacy thing."

"It's the way it is."

"I'd like to write about this Carillo legacy, but there's gotta be conflict for an interesting story. There's no conflict in your family."

"Not now, anyway. We like it this way better."

"But it won't sell books. Hey! I know! Oh, no...never mind."

"What?"

"If Ramone didn't want to live there, then does Victor get it?"

"Yeah."

"That's it! Victor could make Ramone have an "accident" like Gina in Vegas."

"That's terrible! I wouldn't read it."

"It's fiction...a novel. People love a good murder mystery with money involved."

"Well don't put me in that one," Maria grumbled.

They turned down a residential street that ended in

a cul-de-sac three short blocks away. Under a street light, Stark stopped to kneel and tie his shoestrings. Before he stood, Maria looked down at him. When his eyes looked up at her, she could see that his right brown eye was alive and lit with shards of light emanating from its center; like a diamond, it sparkled up at her. Then, she saw that his blue eye was dull and unlit.

"Your brown eye shines so bright."

He explained that his blue eye was the same color as his father's eyes and the brown one was the color of his mother's eyes. He explained that his brown eye had always shone brighter.

"My father was a coal miner who worked awful hard for many years. One day the mine shaft caved in. He rescued twenty-two men who would've died if not for his courage. My mother fell in love with that man, the hero who was willing to sacrifice his life, who saved many from certain death. On their honeymoon my dad lost his arm in a car accident and had to retire with disability. I remember that his eyes were never bright. It was as if they were shut off in some abandoned mine shaft that never saw light."

"That's wild," Maria said.

"Yeah. He believed he was something less than a man after he lost his arm. My mother's eyes were always shining. She said she never wanted me to see her unhappy, so she pretended to be happy for me. But my father's darkness remained and he drank himself to death. My anger at him showed in my blue eye. My brown eye stayed lit for her. I know that sounds totally crazy, but it's true. After he died I thought my blue eye might light up like the other one...but it hasn't."

He could see that Maria was too sweet to say she didn't believe a word of what he just told her.

"What's your real name, Stark?"

"Warren Ellis Starkweather. But don't call me Warren. My parents called me Warren and I hated it."

They headed back for Gina's place. Since Stark was interested in having a Purple 8 session and then writing a book about it, Maria told him that maybe a session would turn his blue eye on.

"Maybe it will," he smiled.

What About Stark?

They were all standing outside Gina's apartment when Robert's truck parked beside Ramone's red convertible. Monica and Robert were delighted to see Gina and the kids. The Ochos could hardly believe their eyes when they saw Gina, now tan and shapely and moving with ease.

"You look fantastic!" Monica squealed after hugging Gina, then Maria. After Robert kissed and embraced Gina, he told Victor and Ramone that the new Gina had to be edited into the end of the documentary.

Ramone introduced Stark to his aunt and uncle then told them that Stark was a writer and that he was writing a novel with Purple 8 in it.

"I'm so glad to meet both of you," Stark said, after shaking their hands. "I would so much like to experience a session. Not only for my book, but for me. I've heard so many incredible things about your formula."

Monica and Robert were impressed with Stark; they explained to him that legally they could only conduct sessions on reservation land.

"Could I come to Ocho Canyon some time soon?" the writer asked.

"Sure," Monica returned.

"Next weekend? The sooner the better for me," Stark pressed.

"I'll go with you," Maria said. "Our bus leaves Monday morning, so as long as I'm back by Sunday night."

"I'll go too!" Victor chimed in. "I want to see my father."

"David's here in Phoenix," Monica said to Victor.

"What's he doing here?" Gina asked, her voice rising with amazement.

"He lives here. He's been here since he quit selling cars. I assumed Richard had told you," Robert said.

"We had no idea he was here," Gina said.

Robert continued, "Monica and I are having dinner with him tonight."

"Gina, have dinner with us," Monica invited with a smile. "It would do David good to see you doing so well."

David lived in a furnished studio apartment just north of Central Avenue in downtown Phoenix. He had remained sober while tending bar at Jack's Place just four blocks from where he lived. He was stunned upon seeing his ex-wife standing outside the downtown restaurant where he had arranged to meet his brother at 7 P.M. Gina was looking better than ever, and David told her that.

During dinner David assured Gina that he didn't want to impose, or bother her and Ramone, now that he was living nearby. Gina told David that Victor was staying with Ramone and going back to finish high school in Omaha soon.

"I know the boys would love to see you. Victor wanted to go to El Centro to see you," Gina said.

"Ramone is making plans to market Purple 8 when the big harvest comes," Robert told his brother.

"And how is Victor? Is he as ambitious as Ramone?"

"He's more of the sensitive artist type," Gina

155

laughed. "He filmed the Purple 8 documentary and really did a great job."

"They are incredible young men," Monica said.

Robert asked, "Dave, have you been tracing?"

"Yes, especially when I'm tending bar. It's really made the difference for me. I use it to keep my mind from wanting to pull me back to my old bad habits. No smoking. No gambling. No drinking," he said proudly.

"How's your social life, David?" Monica asked.

"Oh, I'm not dating. But that's okay. I enjoy my freedom. What about you, Gina? Are you seeing anyone?"

"No, I'm just getting used to the new me," she laughed.

After a very pleasant evening, Gina gave David her and Ramone's phone numbers and urged him to give Victor a call before his son returned to Omaha.

Outside, they all hugged goodbye. Gina watched David walk away. Now Gina knew for certain that the old flame for David had cooled with her restored health. Her only feelings for him now came from a different place, a place that respected the father of Victor and Ramone and the brother of Richard and Robert, two unselfish men who had saved her from a life unlived.

David did call Victor and Ramone the next day, making plans to get together for lunch and then an afternoon Diamondback game at the Bank One Ballpark. That meant that Maria and Stark would go to Ocho Canyon the next weekend.

During the week, Victor hung out with his sister, spending time sunning by the pool and going to coffeehouses and shops around Tempe. He wanted to go back home to the Imperial Valley with Stark and Maria, but wanted to see his father more. He told his sister that he thought Stark really liked her and he wanted to know if his sister was interested in the writer from Carbonville.

"I like him. He's sensitive and intelligent. He let me read a couple of chapters of his book. He's a good writer."

"No, Maria," Victor insisted, "how do you feel about him?"

"I feel like we're friends, just friends."

"I think he's got a thing for you, Sis."

"Did he say anything?"

"No, but I see the way he looks at you. I've been around him enough to know he's really into you."

"Do you think I should go with him this weekend?"

"I wouldn't go alone to Flat Rock, if I were you."

"Oh, you think I'm like Aunt Gina?"

"And Monica and Mom."

"Mom was with Dad at Flat Rock?"

"I can't say for sure, but two outta three is something to keep in mind, if you go to Flat Rock."

They planned on leaving for Ocho Canyon the next day, Friday evening. Stark sensed that Maria was having second thoughts about going alone with him for the weekend. For the past few days, she hadn't been her usual carefree self around him.

"She seems guarded around me lately," Stark told Victor.

"I told her I thought you really liked her."

"Why would you tell her that?"

"Because you do like her."

Stark smiled at his young friend and said, "Look Victor, I do like Maria. Who wouldn't? I'm smart enough to know that it has to be her idea...or rather...she has to be into me—or else nothin's happening. You know what I mean?"

"Not really."

"If a girl isn't interested, then nothing can happen.

So you don't have to worry about your sister with me. I'm not the kind of guy to make moves on just any girl. So she has to be really into me. Sure, Maria is a beautiful girl. It's fun to be around a beautiful girl...that's all."

"She loves to read and she likes your writing. My sister could fall for Stark the writer."

"Are you kidding? She's no dummy, Victor. She knows I'm not much of a ladies man, on or off the page."

Ramone also talked to Maria, after Victor expressed his concern about his sister going alone with Stark to El Centro. Ramone was not one to mince words.

"Why would you even want to go to Ocho Canyon after just seeing Uncle Robert and Aunt Monica?"

"I love that place. I always have," she answered with the same puzzled look that Victor had seen earlier on Stark's face.

"Stark's my friend, but I don't know him well enough for you to be alone with him for a weekend three hundred miles away."

"Mone, what are you saying?"

"I'm saying I don't want you to go alone with Stark to El Centro. I can't stop you from going, but I can cancel my plans this weekend and go with you, if that's what it takes."

"Mone, what is it with you and Victor? I'm almost eighteen."

"Almost is not eighteen."

"Is there something you know about Stark that I should know?"

"No." Ramone shook his head.

"I don't need a bodyguard, Mone. I can take care of myself. What are you guys afraid of?"

"Never mind then. Just forget it. Go with Stark

alone. He works with me. I guess I can trust him with my cousin. I'm sorry, but Victor got me thinking negative stuff."

Ramone hugged Maria and that was the end of it.

A Dust Storm with a Brain Freeze

Next evening around seven, Victor and Ramone watched from the apartment patio as Maria got into Stark's car and left for El Centro. Stark had wanted to leave when the sun was low and metro Phoenix traffic was down from Friday's rush hour. And on top of that, his A/C didn't work, and the temperature had topped 112 degrees during the afternoon.

Maria had called Monica to let her know they were leaving Phoenix at seven and to expect them around midnight.

"I hope that's not too late?"

"Oh no, we'll be up and happy to see you anytime you get here," Monica said with her usual sweetness.

Before they reached I-10, Stark handed his passenger a stack of paper, some fifty pages of his novel.

"It's another version of *Places*. I want you to read this revised version before we get to Ocho Canyon. It'll take about an hour."

Curious, she started to read.

The beginning of his book was about a Navajo family living outside Gallop, New Mexico, in the foothills, in an adobe house on land they bought in 1876. The matriarch of the Viega family knew the value of the purple cactus that only grew on Viega soil. So, she bought more and more land around her until, by the time she died, the entire vast stretch of foothills flanking northeast Gallop was known by locals as Viega Madre.

The healing powers of the purple cactus were similar to Purple 8, except for one thing: it only worked on women. Marie Viega, 17, a fictional character similar in appearance to Maria Carillo, had one brown eye and one blue eye. And this Marie Viega was next in line to inherit the Viega land. The Viega family expected a booming harvest in 2008. The formula patented by her great-grandmother was called Purple 8.

Like the Carillo legacy, Marie Viega also had to marry, but her husband had to be Navajo, or else she could not inherit or live on Viega Madre. That's where the big conflict began, for she was in love with a young white man named John Duffy, who worked in his father's bank in downtown Gallop. This twist in the plot bothered Maria as she read the story, because John was so similar to Alberto.

John and Marie were in love and both were still virgins. She was afraid of getting pregnant and losing everything, including her family, who would surely banish her from Gallop, if she were to have an illegitimate child.

There was another familiar element in the story. Ever since the white man's 'democracy' took over the New Mexico territory, the males in the Viega family began making the laws in their family. The feminine side of the once balanced Navajo Nation was subjugated by the aggressive European maleness of things: land ownership; laws made by men in power who exploited natural resources; and, a new religion ruled by a warlike male God who sacrificed his only son, so that any future sacrifices justified the means, which included war, and the devaluation of women.

And yet these three chapters were filled with beautiful description of the land surrounding Gallop. That's what impressed Maria most about Stark's writing; he had captured a place like Ocho Canyon with all its brutal splendor.

One such place was located behind Viega Madre on the far side of a butte, where a creek called Lost River ran. This water source was the reason a big harvest was predicted in 2008, for every thirty years Lost River would dry up and channel all its water under the Viega Madre ground. *It was a natural phenomenon as intriguing as the history of the Navajo Nation*, Stark wrote.

The hopeless romantic, Maria Carillo, relished the scene where Marie and John walked together barefoot in the mineral rich Lost River, holding hands and joking about solving their dilemma in cynical, humorous dialog. *"I could dye my hair black, visit a tanning salon and change my name to Juan," John laughed.*

But the reading of the last chapter was interrupted by a sudden darkness.

"Oh crap! A dust storm!" Stark complained. "I'd better pull over. Roll up your window."

Stark parked off the shoulder on the desert. They waited it out as violent winds blew dust in a gritty, tan blizzard that threatened to peel the paint off his car. He turned on the dome light and waited while Maria finished reading his pages in the car's hot interior.

She put the stack of paper on her lap and answered him when he asked her what she thought. "I really like it. I care about the characters and want to know what happens to John and Marie."

"You can tell she's not you, right?"

"Yeah, but I read it like she was me," she smiled.

"That's okay. Do you like my voice, my style of writing?"

"Yes, it's interesting and moves along without

details that bore me, like in some books." She stared out at the dust storm. "How long do you think this will last?"

"Should blow over soon."

Stark reached back onto the back seat floor and handed Maria a plastic container of water that they shared.

She wiped her mouth on the sleeve of her t-shirt and asked, "Do you have a bunch of questions to ask my uncle about his formula?"

"Oh yeah! But, see, in my book I had the idea that the Viega Madre land would become the site of a Navajo casino called Purple 8, and that's where Marie could sell her family's formula legally.

"What about John and Marie?"

"Well, I had the idea that John's father's bank provides the finances for the casino and they stay involved. The theme of the book, so far, is not about John and Marie becoming lovers. It's about getting what you want, without hurting anybody who loves you. I don't know. I'm still early in the storyline and I see truckers parked at that casino. I want Purple 8 to do good things for truckers, things that make a real difference. That's what Ramone wants."

"I know."

"I'm writing this for truckers. I just have to tie it all together. The world is really going crazy over oil. I believe truckers will be hit hard by a permanent energy crisis that forces us back to moving goods by rail. Ramone told me that his dad said the truckers are the last American cowboys and they will be extinct, just as sure as the oil will run out one day. Maybe Purple 8 can help truckers move to a better place, find a new way of making a living."

The blowing dust diminished enough for Stark to hit the road again, but at a reduced speed. A few miles later they decided to exit I-8, enticed by a billboard advertising date shakes.

They found a café across from a gift shop/gas station. Both places sold date shakes. They decided to sit out the rest of the storm in a café booth, and watch what locals called a brownout. Maria took a sip of her shake then cracked up when Stark made a tortured face and yelled, "Brain freeze!"

Suddenly, he became thoughtful. "What if Robert put his formula in a shake?" Stark asked.

"It would be easier to take," she agreed. "That's not a bad idea."

"Ask your uncle. It sure sounds easier to market. Hey! I know! Purple 8 Shakes Sold Here!"

"Purple Shakes!" Maria laughed.

"Purple DQ!" Stark proclaimed and laughed with her.

Back on I-8 headed west, the wind blew here and there, but not enough to produce another dust storm as they chased the setting sun.

Closing in on Yuma, Maria asked Stark to explain the book title again.

"Well, it's like...no matter where you go, you can still be in the same place. Like when you get stuck with a label as a kid...that you're slow or dumb, or smart or a geek...or whatever. It can be a place your family gave you."

"A label?"

"Yeah, sometimes. Like Ramone, he has a place he inherits from the family legacy. I don't mean the physical place, Ocho Canyon, but a place reserved in the family, something they expect of him. Like Victor has a place as the artistic one, who ranks below Ramone in age, and so he's second in line for the legacy. They both have a place."

"I don't see my place."

"Your place is the only daughter in this Carillo

164

generation. Your place is to go to college and help make Victor successful."

"How's that?"

"Because if you succeed, Victor must. Your success will motivate him to succeed, or he will be stuck in the terrible middle, the place that gets beaten from both sides."

"I never looked at it that way. That's so interesting, Stark. Places," she said out loud.

"As for me, my place is the only son of a coal miner. I was taught to struggle, to get by, and to survive another day. That's the place I've always had inside me. And unless I get rid of it, through some kind of miracle like Purple 8, I will always be just this slug with a sad past."

They Look Good Together

It was full-dark by the time Stark stopped for gas in Yuma, and for him the journey was about to get darker. Maria made a phone call from the pay phone. Stark was pretty sure he knew who she was calling. It had to be the guy Victor and Ramone had told him about, the guy she liked from Yuma, the vice president's son on whom he had modeled his character John.

It didn't take long to find out. After Stark paid for the gas, Maria informed him that a friend was coming to say hi to her. "I hope you don't mind waiting a few minutes," she added.

Alberto parked his Corvette in front of the pay phones where Maria had said she'd be waiting. Stark watched them embrace and talk excitedly to each other, as if they were thrilled to be reunited. This was exactly the kind of thing that made him feel like that slug with a past, who would always be trailing and leaving his slime for the beautiful people like Maria and Alberto to avoid.

Stark just sat there in his poormobile waiting for the beautiful people to finish their romantic rendezvous. From there he could tell that Alberto was of Latin descent; he was clean-cut, dark and handsome like Victor. And he was probably a bit older than Maria.

Now, Stark felt stupid for feeling jealous. So, as Ramone had taught him, he traced. Tracing his swirling

166

purple 8 gave him his first opportunity to test tracing against such a strong negative feeling.

For perhaps fifteen minutes he concentrated on the figure-8, even getting out of his car to check his oil and clean the dust from all the glass. It was working. Ramone was right, it did help quiet his mind. Yet he was aware that some kind of energy was working within his brain. He let it grow. Awareness came quickly. Thoughts of betrayal were there, telling him over and over that Maria had used him only to hitch a ride in order to see this boy.

He asked his mind where these jealous thoughts came from, because his mother had always been loyal to his father. He'd never had a serious girlfriend, so there was no past pain from a lost love that was making him feel this way.

Stark stopped tracing when he got behind his wheel again, and focused on Maria and Alberto, who were standing close together, chatting like lovers reunited. He told himself that they looked good together. Then, he saw them embrace and kiss goodbye. It was not a first kiss. It was a single long kiss that said she liked him.

She came running over to Stark's car, as Alberto drove away.

"Who was that?" Stark asked casually.

"Alberto. I met him one summer."

"Was he surprised to hear from you?"

"Yeah."

"What kind of work does he do?"

"He works for his dad's credit union."

Minutes later they were waved on by officers at the California border inspection station. Maria was excited by her visit with Alberto and the plans they had made to meet at The Jupiter at noon on Sunday. It was just as she dreamed years ago when they agreed to someday meet

167

there.

She wanted to talk about Alberto with Stark, but there was something that stopped her—a palpable awkwardness loomed between them ever since they left Yuma. Maria had always been able to pick up negative energy and let it pass right through her. This time it was more difficult to do in the confines of Stark's old car.

Stark broke the silence by playing music on the car radio, but the loud music didn't bother her. She was thinking about Alberto. He'd said that he wrote several letters to her and mailed them to the theater in Omaha. Amazed, she told him that she never received a single letter from him.

Now, she was thinking that her father always got all the mail at work, how the mailman always handed the mail to him, or left it on his desk if he wasn't there. The image of her father reading her mail, or tossing it, made her stomach ache.

There was no tracing for Maria Carillo. Purple 8 had never interested her; she'd had no need for it. She had always been 'the good girl' who was truly happy on the inside because her parents trusted her. And now, for the first time in her life, she felt betrayed.

The good girl turned her head to face the Imperial Sand Dunes slicing past the open window, the dark mounds of sand lit here and there by ATV headlights that shimmered. It had been her father's idea to leave Blake; it had been his decision that uprooted them to the frigid north. Reflecting back, her father had made the move about the time she and the boys went to Flat Rock, that magical time when they all made their wishes while sitting inside the purple 8, and when Uncle David was about to be released from prison. My father loves me, I know that, she told herself and sighed deeply.

"So, are you going to see Alberto again?" Stark asked.

"Sunday. I told him I'd meet him at The Jupiter, the theater my dad used to manage in El Centro. I was going to ask you if you could give me a ride. I don't think I want my aunt and uncle to know I'm meeting him."

"Why not?"

"I just don't want them to know."

"Is Alberto a Mexican?"

"Latino. And yes, his family is from Mexicali."

"You seem to really like him."

She smiled. "Yes, I do like him."

"That's good." Stark lied, because he had just muttered to himself, "Lucky bastard."

Mustard on Apples

Robert and Monica were most happy to see their guests. Stark was covered in sweat from the hot desert drive and took a shower right away. They all enjoyed ginger iced tea on the cool and breezy back patio after Stark joined them in frayed cut-off shorts and sleeveless t-shirt; he was carrying a notebook.

"Stark!" Robert greeted his guest. "Come tell us about your writing."

Maria left to shower and Stark gulped down a tall glass of tea, while Robert held his chin with one hand.

Stark had never seen such shining eyes when he looked at Robert. "I want to know more about Purple 8," Stark blurted. "I need to know more about the Carillo legacy for the novel I'm writing. Ramone's tales have intrigued me. I want to write about Purple 8 and to help market it to truckers. I usually write solitary observations that nobody will ever read. But when Ramone told me about the harvest in 2008, I could see the story developing, something that interested me enough to write about."

"And you want to help people," Robert stated.

"The way I see it...if Purple 8 helps me...it can help others...and that makes the world a better place."

"Most writers write about their own experiences," Monica said.

"Yes, I suppose they do. Or else it wouldn't

170

interest them. That's why I want to experience Purple 8. Ramone and Gina both told me how much it improved their lives after having one of your sessions. Ramone mentioned that you changed your formula."

"Yes! It's much less dramatic. Now the elimination of toxins occurs during regular bowel movements," Robert said.

Stark began taking notes.

"The results are the same, but happen over a longer period of time," Monica added.

"Gina was right when she called it purple crap!" Robert declared, and they all laughed.

"The formula is still in liquid form?" Stark asked.

"Yes, twelve ounces for adults. I hope to produce it in capsule form, but probably not for some time," Robert said, while his guest scribbled in his notebook.

"When's the best time to take it?"

"On an empty stomach in the morning. I suggest fasting for 72 hours after taking it. Are you willing to do that?" Robert gazed at Stark expectantly.

"Yes, I can write about how I feel during that time. Can I take it tomorrow on Flat Rock?"

Robert and Monica laughed, explaining that it was not necessary to take the session there, that the rock had been a private place to go when the formula was more radical.

"What time tomorrow?"

"When you get up." Monica smiled.

"So you can show me the blue cactus and Flat Rock tomorrow?"

"Sure," Robert promised.

Stark found it difficult to fall asleep. He was so excited about the upcoming session, and also disappointed knowing that Maria was going to be seeing Alberto on Sunday. She was so full of life, not in the least jaded, a fantasy girl he'd never seen the likes of back home.

And yes, starting tomorrow he would start his new life, inside his mind and body, and perhaps that would erase his lingering sense of betrayal. It was a feeling that he knew was irrational for a girl with whom he had no emotional history whatsoever.

Meanwhile, Maria was under the covers in the other guest room, buoyed with romantic images of her date with Alberto on Sunday: holding hands when they walked together; kissing in his parked car under the shade of palm trees in the city park while listening to soft music; and then the two of them on Flat Rock at sunset. She imagined Alberto holding her against his chest while he whispered to her what he wrote in his lost letters.

Stark was awakened Saturday morning by the smell of fresh coffee. He dressed quickly and was greeted by his hosts in the kitchen. On the clean counter there was a slender 12-ounce crystal glass full of purple liquid that foamed at the top with crackling aliveness.

"This is for me?" he asked bleary eyed.

"Enjoy," Robert said and smiled.

"Coffee sounds good, too," Stark said.

"You can have coffee or any other liquid with it. But drink it all," Monica directed.

He emptied the glass quickly, leaving a purple ring around his lips, whereupon Monica handed her guest a napkin. "It does taste good, kinda sweet," he said. "But the texture is sort of weird."

Monica poured, then handed Stark a cup of coffee. Robert reminded him that he could eat if he wanted to, but that the formula was much more effective if he fasted.

"For 72 hours?"

"Right."

"Then, I won't eat."

Over coffee Robert told Stark they could go out into the canyon before it got too hot. Stark went to retrieve his notebook and bumped into Maria coming out of her room. She greeted him, "Good morning."

"I've already taken Robert's formula," Stark announced.

"Good."

He walked with her into the kitchen, asking her if she wanted to go with them into the canyon. She declined.

Stark couldn't keep his eyes off Maria. She wore a long black t-shirt and nothing else that he could see. Her wild black hair was full of curls. She had no makeup at all on her face. She was the most beautiful girl he'd ever laid eyes on.

Stark followed Maria outside to the back patio. As she sipped her coffee, he wrote furiously in his notebook; they were words about her. And now as she scanned the distant canyon walls that were the color of cinnamon in the morning light, he wrote:

> *She closed her dreamy brown eyes when she drank from her cup; then she opened them lazily after she'd had a sip. Her attention was on this place of her ancestors, on the canyon walls that her people must have gazed upon a hundred thousands mornings like this. Except I was with her, a white man over four years older and three shades*

lighter.

Her uncle will soon be taking me beyond these canyon walls to see and learn more about her people. I want her to go with me, partly because, when I learn about things connected to her family, I want her to see me taking it all in, partly due to ulterior motives that I fear I have.

Why must the things I truly want seem to be so unreachable. Though I have ingested the juice of her peoples' blue cactus just minutes ago, I hope its effects do not eliminate the attraction I have for her. However, if it does, I hope I can accept it and become a better writer because of it.

I want to ask her to go with us to see the blue cacti, because I know that her presence will inspire me to capture things on paper that can only enhance 'Places.'

To be a writer is to live like one. If I am ready, make this formula bring me to that place I have desired for so many years. Until I can string the right words together on paper, I'll be a hack, an amateur unable to want success badly enough to make it real. Purple 8 is real; I can already feel it changing things inside me. This feeling is mixed with sincere hope that the formula will remove emotional toxins that I know lie dormant inside my body in a thousand places.

It's those kind of places that I want to write about, places that are charged with old emotions that have kept me unwilling to admit that I'm vulnerable, place that have held my energy down much too low to live my life to its full potential. I know a higher energy will keep me from repeating the lives of my parents, and will bring me compassion and laughter instead of anger and resentment, grief and disease that could one day attack my heart and kill me like it killed my father.

So I want a happy Saturday for me. Since I realize my reality is what I reflect—I pray for the highest human energy possible without delay so that I have a chance with Maria.

Just then, Robert came outside dressed for the summer desert, wearing sunglasses, a wide-brimmed straw hat with a narrow band of purple around it, faded khaki shorts, a faded green, long sleeve cotton shirt, and rugged, dusty hiking boots. He carried a tall hickory walking stick.

175

He handed Stark one of the two canteens of water draped over his burly shoulder.

"Do you have a hat I can borrow?" Stark asked his guide.

In seconds Robert returned with another hat identical to his, except it was more careworn. Maria called out, "See you later!"

Robert led the way into the canyon. Stark stayed a few steps behind his guide, scribbling notes of things he noticed. One of the things on the path was the curled skin shed by a rattlesnake that looked exactly like the covering around Robert's canteens.

"Lots of snakes out here, huh?"

"Not so many. Snakes are not fond of the blue cactus. They do not like to live too close to this area. They move on."

"Why is that?" Stark asked while writing.

"I can't prove it, but my father told me when I was a boy that the juice from the blue cactus will kill them if it touches their skin."

"Why's that?"

"I don't know. Somehow it messes with their nervous system. That's what I think, but I can't prove it."

Robert pointed out Flat Rock up ahead on the right. But they hiked on, moving past the place he'd heard so much about from Ramone and Victor. They went deeper into the canyon where, suddenly, dry gusts of wind came swirling from many directions and cooled them under the hot sun on the open desert path. They were still about a hundred yards from shady spots cast by canyon walls which rose forty feet high in places.

When they turned past the canyon's left flank, Stark saw the blue cactus. He removed his sunglasses so he could see their true color. They were a jade-gray, and not at all the blue he had imagined. Each one stood alone, the bigger ones at least eight feet tall with massive orbs in the shape of figure-8s. As they neared, it seemed to Stark that the larger cacti were protecting the younger ones, like a herd of buffalo, the adults keeping the young in the center. From a distance, what had appeared like a hundred cacti grew tenfold as they neared the 'baby blues' rising out of the desert earth.

"This is the harvest?" he asked his guide. Robert nodded yes and took a drink from his canteen, which prompted Stark to do likewise. He thought he better ask Robert a few things before he forgot the questions that seemed to come and go in the numbing heat. "Why do they only grow here?"

"They grow in Mexico, too, but only thrive here. It's because of climate, and a peculiar thing I realized one day. You know how some people only thrive in one place? If you take them away from their place, they seem to not do well."

"Yes! We all have our places," the writer smiled, trying to get down every word just as he heard it.

"Well," Robert said, "this is the place of the blue cactus."

Within twenty minutes they were seated on the shaded back half of Flat Rock, their backs against the canyon wall and their hats and sunglasses tossed aside. A breeze came often and cooled them as Robert explained that by fasting for 72 hours after taking his formula, Stark would experience one final elimination that would carry the most toxins, and that it would actually be purple.

Both sipped from their canteens.

"I was looking forward to having a session here...the old way, spilling my rotten past on Flat Rock like Ramone did."

"This way is much better for everyone," Robert said.

"Robert, this story I'm writing tells how difficult it can be to escape a place a family gives to each of their own. Do you know what I mean by 'a place'? I mean...I know you understand it...what I really want to know is if that kind of place, whether instilled or inherited, will change after the purple crap in 72 hours? Gina and Ramone both seem to be in a better place, compared to the way they said they used to be."

"You're right. You're talking about something that keeps thousands and thousands of kids your age in what I call 'emotional prison.' I see it every place I go. It depends on your parents. If they were unconscious about assigning you your place, then Purple 8 can help you escape it, provided you trace and give it attention. Purple 8 will help your body eliminate toxins that upset the chemical balance. It's up to you to keep the toxins from returning."

"How can I do that?"

"Trace a purple 8 in your imagination instead of letting your mind chatter. Some of my clients visualize the figure-8 in a peaceful setting."

"That's what Gina does. I think Ramone does, too, sometimes. Ramone explained how to trace and I've tried it a little here and there."

Robert replied, "You have to quiet your mind and monitor your mind's chatter, or you'll just fall back into old habits. That's what I tell everyone who takes the formula. It only works if you learn to take back the power you have surrendered to your mind."

"Oh, God, Robert I so want that! I want it now, instantly, without anymore waiting or suffering. I learned suffering from my parents. It's the kind of suffering I could hear those self-righteous people talking about back home at my dad's funeral: "We all prayed for a miracle and God delivered us through Lefty Starkweather;" "At least he's not suffering now." I wanted to scream at all of them: "Yeah, he's not suffering now...because he's dead...you morons! Some white-bearded God wasn't looking down on Carbonville, when mine shaft 99 caved in! My old man was!" My dad said he didn't want to die in hell any more than those trapped men did. And after he lost his arm on his honeymoon, both my parents went straight to hell and tried to see just how much suffering they could endure."

Robert was smiling, for he knew his formula was working, releasing pent up emotions the young writer had been holding onto. And Stark realized just that, when he stopped his ranting and observed, "I sound like a whining child who wants everything in the candy store. I don't usually go on like this unless I'm writing."

"It's part of your release. The formula only works when you are focused on eliminating those poisonous emotions. That's why tracing your purple 8 is important. It will keep your mind still and let your body heal itself. Be ready, Stark, to welcome changes, because they are inevitable."

"Good changes?"

"Yes, if you choose to see them as good."

Stark began to laugh.

"What's so funny?" Robert asked.

"I can see I should be tracing now. For some reason my mind was showing me an image of my dad. He liked to put mustard on apples. I tried it once and spit if out fast. I never thought of that until now."

"That is your mind resisting your desire to quiet it," Robert smiled.

"Yes, I see that."

Robert fell quiet; he could tell that Stark was tracing while gazing off at the canyon.

A few minutes later, Stark opened his notebook and asked Robert several questions about the Carillo legacy.

"I'd like to use the legacy in my story. I mean...I'm writing about a family in Gallop, New Mexico, like yours, and they have the blue cactus. I have a hard time writing anything but fiction. Still, your legacy and the formula is such a good foundation for a story."

"I don't care what you write, if it helps promote the formula. You are the author and you'll write what you want. However, to market Purple 8, I believe you should write nonfiction using real names and places. People like to read about real people."

"I couldn't even write about my own family let alone someone else's. I just don't know."

"Whatever, I look forward to reading it."

"I'll make sure you get a chance to read it before it is published. Ramone said he might publish it for me."

"Yeah, he told me."

"Ya know, it's interesting about Ramone, Victor and Maria. They are all so different from each other, even though they were raised together."

"That's because they each have a different mother."

"I never thought of that. Victor's mother is the unknown in your family. A fictional character like Victor would have the most conflict going on, because he doesn't know his real mother."

"Yes, and he might be better off not knowing her. That's what I hope he believes," Robert said.

"Yes, I can understand that...but if the character believed just the opposite, it would add a lot of conflict in my story."

Robert watched Stark's left hand moving with each

letter across his page, the writer's head craned down in utmost attention. Robert knew that work on his book would be a challenge for the young man over the next few days while the formula continued to attack the toxins in Stark's body.

Stark believed that if he kept writing it would diminish the physical and emotional affect of fasting. Now, he was writing about Robert's beautiful niece and how he felt about her going to meet Alberto the next day. He truly believed that by allowing himself to think he was in love with Maria, he could capture the love interest he needed in his book. So, he wrote about his fantasy in clipped sentences:

> *I will be the one to deliver her to the handsome kid from Yuma. Easy to love her. Any man would who first saw her. Very hungry for her. Would be easy to take her away from all others, drive her to Mexico and never return. With her overprotective family out of the picture, I know she would begin to love me in time. I need time alone with her. She will see that I can take care of her as well as her family can. Tomorrow. Dread. Loss.*

Hunger

By late Sunday morning Stark was hungrier than he'd ever been in his life. Orange juice and coffee sloshed in his grumbling belly while he waited in his car for Maria to come out after saying goodbye to her aunt and uncle. She hadn't mentioned her date with Alberto.

When he saw her come out the front door carrying her black tote bag—she was definitely dolled up for her date, in white shorts, a baby blue t-shirt and butterscotch sandals; passion red lipstick covered her full lips. When she first got inside his car he smelled the sweet scent of her perfume in her thick black hair.

He began to trace when his mind accused, "She wouldn't wear perfume for you...only for the rich boy from Yuma."

They drove away, waving goodbye to the Ochos, who stood smiling and waving outside their front door.

"Thanks for not mentioning my date with Alberto."

"No problem."

Once onto the narrow dirt road that led to the eastern border of the reservation near Nine Palms, four miles away, she told Stark that she would not be with Alberto for more than a few hours and asked if he could pick her up at The Jupiter at three.

Looking at her watch she said that they had time to stop at Blake. She wanted to see her old home. "Can we stop there for a few minutes?"

"Sure. I'd like to see it. It might help me with my Gallop scenes in Places."

"Places is your title?"

"So far, it is."

When he drove by Nine Palms she said, "This is where Robert will session locals, the ones he doesn't want to come to Ocho Canyon. We used to have picnics here and play cards with the adults. We had so much fun. How are you doing? You must be so hungry."

"I'm okay. Just one more day and I can eat again."

"You are brave to do this for your book. That means that you're committed to your writing."

"Yeah."

Then he picked up his tracing when his cynical mind said, "I wish you were committed to me."

They crossed over the canal and cruised along the gravel road that ran in front of Blake. Maria was ruminating about the many times she rode the school bus on this obscure road. Some of the old shacks, homes of poor Mexican families, showed familiar signs of life: clothes hanging out to dry on a clothesline, rusting vehicles parked nearby, chained dogs panting in shaded places, and an overwhelming feeling that this was a place where a family could remain together and survive in a new world of hope.

Stark parked his old car near the center of Blake in front of the fourth door from the left. The door had a faded welcome mat and a black mailbox that marked it as the entrance.

"Looks like you each had your own door."

"We rarely used the other doors."

"Where was your room?"

He followed her along the exterior of Blake as she pointed out each room from Gina's on the far left to the other end of the building where her parents' bedroom had been. He peered into a few of the front windows and could see that the main room was furnished with an old, blanket-covered couch and some tables that David had used.

Just above the front door Maria felt for the spare key that had always been kept there. She couldn't reach that high so Stark slid his hand across the ledge and soon found a key and handed it to her.

The interior of Blake was very hot. Maria gave Stark a quick tour, going from room to room, showing him places that brought back so many good memories for her.

When Stark returned the key to its hiding place, he told her that Ramone wanted to sell Robert's formula there. She showed little interest in the plan. She wanted to be on time to meet Alberto.

They spoke few words on the way to The Jupiter, except for Maria's driving directions.

Alberto's red corvette was parked in front of the theater.

"See you at three," she told Stark and bolted from his car. He stayed parked near the Corvette until it sped off, leaving Jupiter like a red rocket. He scribbled in his notebook the personalized Arizona license plate 'REDVET' and wrote that the color of the vette was the same color as Maria's lipstick. His heart ached. He wrote:

I wanted to follow them because I don't trust that guy with the fancy car...and with the girl of my dreams. If he ever harmed a hair on her beautiful head I would hunt him down and leave his body to rot in the desert. I'm so hungry right now...I could eat him alive.

Three

Near I-8, after filling his car with gas and buying a pack of gum, Stark decided to go west on the interstate to see if there were any good billboard locations for Ramone's Purple 8 marketing plan.

He drove all the way to the Blake exit, pretending to be interested in outdoor advertising. He had to take the exit or climb deep into the mountains and waste expensive fuel. Even before he reached the end of the exit's ramp, he could see the REDVET parked at Blake. She had taken him there.

He had to turn right and pass Blake. No way was he going to stop and intrude on their privacy. So he parked a few hundred yards away where he could still see the front of Blake and the parked vette.

He began to write, taking swigs from his water jug.

> *No shade here. Must be 120 degrees in my car. Maria has taken Alberto to Blake. I am parked here, not far away from Blake, making sure she is safe. I was surprised to see his REDVET parked at Blake. I did not follow them here. If he leaves Blake without her I will rush to her aid. It's so hot, I can't imagine them*

*staying in there long. Oh God, I
wish I had driven her back to
Phoenix, then this would not be
happening. I would be halfway to
Phoenix by now. God, it's hot.*

After an interminable half hour he started his car
and drove over to Nine Palms, the closest spot with any
shade at all that he could see.

His body cooled considerably after he poured water
from his jug onto his face and bare chest. Purposely, he lay
on his back on the earth stained by Purple 8. His eyes
fluttered with the rustling hypnotic sound of the fan-
shaped leaves high above him in the desert oasis. His
notebook was within reach if he needed it. Hunger was at
its peak now, because he usually ate lunch about this time.

Repulsive images came to him, images of Maria
with Alberto on that couch in Blake. At three, he thought,
she would return to The Jupiter as Alberto's girl, and she
would always be thinking of and wanting to be with that
slick pretty boy from Yuma, instead of me.

Upon realizing his mind was hurting him and
draining his energy—he traced, sweeping his body from
head to toe with a giant purple 8. It kept fading until he used
the memory of Robert's purple hat band as a visual image
that kept his 8 purple. Then wider and wider he made
his purple 8, until it was wide enough to cover nearly every
inch of the encircling palm trees. Longer and longer he held
its purple swirl without changing directions, each minute
seeming like an eternity, because his mind had never been
resisted like this—ever. The urge and refusal to go into his
head to hash things over and over about Maria was
painfully mixed with hunger. But then he chose to see the
geraniums potted in clay on the back patio at Ocho

Canyon. He had noticed them when he returned from Flat Rock with Robert. He really saw them for the first time, their thick green leaves glowing with vitality, solid proof for him that the formula was working.

He continued tracing until he nodded off into a nap that was just long enough for a quick dream. He opened his eyes and made himself remember the dream before it was lost forever in the cluster of green shade so high above him. He reached for his notebook without moving his eyes, in a half-waking state of lost dreams in the desert, and wrote as fast as he could.

> *My eyes were one color. They were blue like my father's. I was with Maria on the sidewalk of downtown Carbonville. I was walking with her and we were holding hands. I wanted to show her off to anyone back home who saw us together. I kept hoping that everyone I saw was someone who knew me. But nobody did. Each person was a stranger. When we turned to face a sidewalk window, the reflection was that of my father and mother when they were young, before they married. They had happy faces then, like mine would be with Maria.*
>
> *If there is a God, some old and wise, white-bearded creator who decides who we get to be with—put Maria in this life for*

me. Give me this girl of my dreams, God, or take her out of my mind now, before something happens.

He drank more water and looked at his watch. Still over an hour to go. From here he could see only the back of Blake, unable to see if the vette was still there.

Again he closed his eyes. This time he traced his purple 8 in his belly and held his attention there. His hunger subsided and some kind of knowing that he would be alright filled his body with waves of tingling energy.

For nearly an hour he kept up his tracing, willing himself to stay with it. It was easier to see that his mind had been in charge of his reality. Clearly, now, he knew that Robert's formula was certainly something good—but could never be mass-marketed to the public.

He wrote:

I have bad news for Ramone. His dream to become rich when the harvest comes will fail. Not because of the product, but rather because of the fearful nature of people. Oh, here and there will be people like me and Ramone, who believe in it, but that's a far cry from the number of people it would take to make us rich. I now believe Purple 8 is meant to give the keeper of Ocho Canyon a peaceful way to live among the fearful herd. The Carillo family and those fortunate few close to them, like me, will reap the benefits of the harvest.

Truth has to come out. I can see now that I led Ramone on by telling him that I could help his dream by writing a novel that promotes Purple 8. My intention was good in my old state of mind, before trying his uncle's new formula. And I know that when I met Maria I hyped my intentions more by writing things just to win her approval. I admit there is no novel in me...at least about Purple 8. Now that I see the kind of guy that Maria wants—I have lost my desire to write about the girl I can never have in a million years of useless scribbling.

When I return to Phoenix, I want to tell Ramone that I was using him in order to be a part of his dream and near his beautiful cousin. Ramone is the first person I have ever tried to know. I hope he will remain my friend when I tell him these things.

Or perhaps I will leave him a letter at work, explaining that, after I saw Maria with Alberto, I could not be around her or her family anymore. I promised Maria I would not tell anyone she was with Alberto, her secret

*lover. But I am her true secret
lover...Ramone ought to know
that. At three, I will pick her up at
The Jupiter and see if she has
betrayed me. If she has...I will
have to let her go. Alberto will be
in her heart for a very long time.
I fear he has ruined her and will
destroy the sweet person she is.*

He tore out the pages he'd written since leaving
Phoenix with Maria. Then he flipped his thick notebook
back to the first page and read the words he had copied
there. It was a quote about places from one of Zane Grey's
novels. He added Grey's words to the torn pages and folded
them in half.

From the trunk of his car he brought a hammer back
to the Purple 8 stain he'd been lying on and he began
clawing up the desert earth three inches deep, until he could
bury the pages and cover them. Then he poured water on the
earth to seal it before he stomped on the spot and leveled it
smooth with his sandal.

He had buried his words because he could never
hurt Ramone by telling him his truth on paper. Nine Palms,
a place on the Carillo family's reservation would hold his
truth forever.

When he drove past Blake the vette was gone. At the
ramp entrance to I-8 East, he stopped and made a U-turn.
Stark drove fast before he changed his mind. Quickly, he
parked near the front door and found the key. Before he
went inside Blake, he traced, to quiet the chattering weasel
that was telling him to invade Maria's secret place.

Two things assaulted his sense of smell when he
stepped inside: the aroma of marijuana and the sweet scent

of Maria's perfume as he moved closer to the old couch. He stood over it and told himself that they only sat there and talked and, at the most, they kissed. And then she kissed for the last time and pushed him away telling him no further. Then she explained that she was different from other girls and that his good looks and fancy car were not going to make her do anything more.

Yes, that's what happened, Stark told himself. However, he left Blake knowing that the thin blanket that had covered the couch earlier was now gone, leaving the faded beige couch with all its flaws.

At three o'clock, REDVET was idling in the same spot when Stark parked behind it. He couldn't see through the dark tint of the vette's back window.

Soon, Maria got out and Alberto sped off. Like a loser with a big red toy who had been rejected by his girlfriend, Stark hoped, defying reality. He hid behind his sunglasses and studied her body language as she approached his front passenger door. She wasn't smiling. Bad sign. And something about her posture was different. He told himself that it was because she had been sitting on that couch for hours, telling the rich boy "no."

Maria turned to her window and her eyes raked over the old theater, its familiar entrance and single-seat box office exactly as she remembered it. Her dreams of finding real love had begun here. And now, as Stark drove away, Jupiter moved past her glass and vanished.

"How was your date?" he asked.

"Fine," she faked a smile.

"Where'd ya go?"

She reached over and turned on the radio. "We went to Blake and talked."

"To Blake? It's hotter than hell in there."

"I opened some windows. It wasn't too bad."

That's what Stark had wanted to hear. She hadn't lied to him.

"What did you do?" she asked.

"Oh, I drove around...took a nap."

"A nap? In your car?"

"No, I went to this place that had shade. I'm so hungry you wouldn't believe it."

"Let's stop again and get another date shake. Uncle Robert said you could have liquids."

"Yeah, that sounds good." He smiled.

A Girl in Trouble

In mid-October Stark gave his two-week notice to John at Tempe Sign and gradually broke the news to Ramone, between phone calls, that he was unable to write any novel, especially the one that Ramone had been counting on to market his dream.

"I don't have it in me, Mone. I thought I did. I realized it when I was fasting at Ocho Canyon. It became clear to me that writing a novel about Purple 8 was beyond me."

Ramone asked him if he'd write a testimonial explaining how his life had changed since taking the formula.

"Sure I can write how I trace at work, and that it helps me at the end of the day, because I'm not holding onto stress like before. I sleep much better. My experiences with Purple 8 have improved my life."

"You going back to Carbonville?"

"Yeah. I figure I'll stay at my mom's place for awhile to save some money. I'm gonna see if she'll try the formula."

"That would be good. Then what'll you do for work?"

"I don't know. Giving up writing might lead me to something.

In Omaha, after her drama class, Maria walked to a

nearby drugstore and bought a pregnancy test kit. At home she found out what she already knew, that she was pregnant.

Ever since she turned eighteen a month ago, when her parents told her that they would support her no matter where she wanted to go to college, she realized she had let them down by doing something really stupid at Blake last summer.

Not once had Alberto called or written her. For weeks she had checked the mail every day after she got home from school. Tonight she would call him and tell him the news. She needed to hear his voice tell her that he had only used her for sex. Now she was certain that he had never sent letters to the theater, like he said he had.

Alone, she went for a long walk in her neighborhood, recounting their reunion in El Centro. The incredible explosion of autumn leaves on trees all around her went unnoticed as she recalled climbing into Alberto's car in front of The Jupiter. "You look beautiful," he had said. Then he leaned over and kissed her. She could smell marijuana on his clothes and on his fingers when he touched her hair. It reminded her of the girls' bathroom at school.

He told her that they only had three hours together, that he almost didn't show because he knew how hard it would be to see her, then not see her again for a long time.

"Can we just go somewhere and talk?" he asked.

"We can go to my old house. Nobody lives there."

He held her hand while he drove along I-8, telling her about his work in his father's credit union. He said that he got two weeks paid vacation every year. He could come visit her when she was in college. "If you want me to?" he grinned with those dark eyes and a boyish charm that made her squeeze his fingers.

Then he charmed her more when he reminded her,

"This is the reunion we promised each other after our first date at The Jupiter." He kissed her fingers. "Now, we're all grown up."

At Blake, she opened several windows to cool the room. Sitting on the old couch they smoked his pipe. She coughed from the harsh smoke. They sat close together, his arm around her, while he talked about the future. His words led her to believe that she would share it with him.

"When I come visit you, I'm going to take you to the best restaurants and we can go dancing; I'll be making enough money to be able to treat you like a princess. I just hope some guy in college doesn't win your heart before we have a chance to see how we are together."

Though it was very hot in Blake, there was a slight cross-breeze, and, after lots of kissing, she let him have her body on that old couch. There was nothing romantic about it at the time, or looking back on it now, as she walked slowly through a universe of confusion and lies. She had nearly puked before he was done. She knew then that this was not the love she had read about, for his face had turned ugly when she begged him to stop, but he wouldn't, until he was finished.

She remembered how he had changed when it was over. His sweetness was gone. The evidence was obvious that he was her first, but it didn't seem to matter. When he put the bedspread into his car trunk and said nothing to her on the drive back to The Jupiter, she knew she had made the biggest mistake of her life. There was no more cuddling, or talk about the future.

She had time to recall the words of a friend at school who had gotten pregnant her junior year, her words ringing loud and clear as the red Corvette raced for The Jupiter. "It's all a girl has and all the boys ever want. We should hang on to it for as long as we can and make it more valuable. The smart ones do, though they are made to feel like it's not normal to hold out. It's always the voices of those that gave it up that weaken you and make you feel like you're missing something, if you don't."

Now as she walked through the fallen autumn leaves, she remembered that she didn't cry about it until she went to bed at Ramone's apartment after she returned with Stark.

Stark. She thought of the time they each drank a second date shake at that obscure exit in the Arizona desert. His words made her smile even now. They had been sipping their shakes seated in a booth facing each other, both wearing sunglasses that hid their eyes from each other.

"Just think," he had said, "this is our second date...shake."

She laughed then, and thought it odd now that she never laughed when she had been with Alberto. Lies don't make you laugh, she thought.

She knew she couldn't tell her parents straight out that she was pregnant. Victor—she could trust her brother to help her tell them—tonight.

After dinner she told Victor that she wanted to go for a walk and talk to him about something. She told him everything, even the details about how Alberto wouldn't stop when she wanted him to.

"Alberto doesn't know?"

"I just found out."

"You've got to tell him. Maybe he'll step up and marry you."

"No, I know he won't," she signed. "Anyway, I won't either. He's a liar."

Victor put his arm around her and told her that Alberto still had to know that he had a baby coming into the world.

"I'm afraid to tell Dad."

"Yeah, he's the one who's gonna be hit hard by this. Are you sure you're pregnant? I mean...you may not be...right?"

"No, I am. Oh, Victor, it's horrible. I've been so stupid!"

"Okay, okay, take it easy. Who will you tell first, Dad or Alberto?"

"I don't know, Victor. Right now I'm so mad at myself for letting this happen to me."

"Yeah...you'd be the last person I'd imagine this happening to. And your first time. It was your first time, right?"

"Yes!"

"And he didn't use protection?"

"No!"

"I'm sorry, Maria, it's just that this is such a shock. But, you know, I've seen girls in your spot...and the ones who stay in school seem to do pretty well."

Maria knew she wasn't going to be free of her anxiety until she talked to Alberto and her father. She asked her brother to not tell Ramone or Gina until she had told Richard.

"Okay, but I know you're gonna be a great mom and soon you'll see that your baby is the best thing that ever happened to you...no matter what Dad and Alberto say."

They stopped and hugged on the sidewalk.

The chill of an early winter had come to Omaha for those who loved Maria. She told her parents that evening, after her walk with Victor. Lola tried to diminish the dread and despair flooding her husband's flushed face by reminding him of the times they thought she was pregnant before they married. Yet Richard left the room brooding over the shocking news. Maria collapsed onto her mother's lap, "Oh, Mother, I've ruined my life, haven't I?" she cried.

"No Maria...not at all, honey. You've only changed your life...a little faster than we wanted it to, that's all," Lola said softly, while stroking her daughter's hair.

"I don't know how I could be so stupid to let this happen to me. I can't go to school pregnant," she sobbed.

"Well, the next thing I suggest you do is call the baby's father."

Maria's phone call to Alberto was short and not at all sweet. Lola stood beside her when she told him she was pregnant with his baby.

"Are you sure I'm the father?"

"Yes."

"Well...what are you going to do about it? Are you going to have it?"

Maria slammed down the phone and fell, sobbing into her mother's arms.

Victor could hear everything, standing outside his sister's bedroom door. It sickened him to hear her crying. He entered Maria's room. "He won't step up?" Victor asked Lola.

She shook her head no and tried to console Maria. "This is your home no matter what, your father and I will support you and the baby."

"He's gotta pay support at least. He can't get away with not supporting his kid!" Victor ranted. "What kind of work does this Alberto do?"

"He works in his dad's credit union in Yuma," Maria sobbed.

"Which one?"

"I don't know."

"He probably lied about that, too. When that baby's born you can prove he's the father with a blood test. You gotta go after that creep, Maria. You can't let him get away with not supporting you and your baby."

A Place Revealed

Victor's phone call came while Stark was at Ramone's apartment. Hearing the unbelievable news about Maria was tough on Ramone. His blood was boiling like his brother's when he relayed the news to Stark.

"I knew that jerk was no good. I shouldn't have taken her to meet him. She asked me not to tell anyone she was with him."

"That bastard got her high on pot and wouldn't stop when she wanted. She wouldn't tell Victor where it happened."

Stark felt he had to tell Ramone what he knew, since his friend was pacing his apartment like a wild man. "Ramone, I know where they went."

Ramone stood staring at Stark as he told him about Maria's date with Alberto. "She called Alberto from Yuma and he came to the gas station and made a date with her that Sunday to meet at The Jupiter. I drove her to the theater where the REDVET was waiting. She got into the car and they drove off. Later, I drove down I-8 looking for billboard locations. I saw his car parked at Blake."

"Why didn't you go in and stop him?"

"I couldn't do that. She'd think I was spying on her. No way was I gonna bust in on them."

"I would've."

"I'm not related to her. She would've thought I was

200

some weirdo."

"Then what happened?"

"I met her at The Jupiter at three like she asked me to. That was it."

"That bastard took advantage of her in her own house. This'll ruin Maria," Ramone lamented to Stark.

"I wish I would've done things different."

Ramone and Stark forgot to trace that night after Victor's call; each was taken over by hostile thoughts because Maria was hurting. This was the time that Robert had said to trace, when things went wrong and answers were far away, and waiting was difficult.

Ramone wanted to drive to Yuma that night and kill that bastard who had raped Maria. Victor had said that Alberto would not stop when Maria wanted to, and that's how she got pregnant. But it was Stark who angered Ramone, when he said that Maria was just as much to blame, because she let Alberto get started.

Then Stark added, "I'm not saying it's right, Mone, I'm just not sure that Alberto's all to blame for this."

Ramone told Stark, "I'm going to the pool, to cool down my thoughts."

In the pool, Ramone decided to go to David to tell him what happened to Maria, thinking maybe his father could help figure out what could be done to help the situation. Ramone Carillo had always protected Maria; he was primed to explode with retribution for the violent way Alberto hurt his cousin.

In bed that night, with the bedroom window open to let in the cool Arizona night air, Ramone cried for Maria. He was assailed by vivid memories of her angelic face lost in a movie as he sat next to her in The Jupiter. He remembered her crying, hoping the girl on the big screen would be rescued by the hero and taken away to a safe place. Even now he could see her profile, her brown eyes wide open as if in wonder and awe of all the magical things she was seeing in her father's movie house.

"I could kill that bastard!" Ramone shouted into his pillow, pounding his fist onto his mattress.

Ramone knew that if he lost his temper he would end up in prison, and that would hurt Maria more than anything he could do to Alberto. He thought of how his generation of Carillos had been spared most of the same drama that David and Gina caused in Las Vegas, until now.

"Poor Uncle Richard," Ramone mumbled before sleep came.

At work the next morning, Stark heard Ramone call his dad and tell him he wanted to talk to him. He told David he would stop by when he got off work.

Stark rode along with Ramone in his convertible. They put the top down and cruised across Phoenix on McDowell Avenue. It was the most perfect weather, the kind of weather that had made the valley one of the fastest growing cities in the country over the last two decades. Ramone played his favorite jazz station turned up loud. They didn't say a word over the forty-minute drive to the bar where David worked as a bartender.

The dark bar was crowded for happy hour, though few patrons looked happy. Most of them were regulars, red-faced alcoholics with swollen red noses and cigarettes burning in one hand.

David came from behind the bar and gave his son a hug before introducing him to Pete, his boss. "Pete, this is my oldest son, Ramone.

Ramone shook Pete's clammy hand, then Ramone introduced Stark. "Dad, this is my friend Stark, he works with me."

"Pleased to meet you," David offered a smile with his handshake. "You boys want something to drink?"

"A Coke."

"Me, too," Stark said.

Stark could see Victor's resemblance to his dad, but could not see any physical features that Ramone had in common with his father.

Pete tended bar while David took the boys over to a booth by the back door where they could talk. He sat across from the boys ready to listen, craning his dark head forward and smiling at his son. He asked, "Ramone, what did you want to talk about?"

"It's Maria. She got pregnant. Her first time and the guy wouldn't stop when she told him to."

David's dark eyes scared Stark; they turned cold and piercing when he spoke. "Are you tellin' me that Maria was raped?"

"I don't know for sure if it was a rape, Dad."

"She let him and then she wanted to stop?" David asked.

"Yeah."

"And no protection?"

"Right."

David shook his head knowing this was going to be tough on his brother. "What did Richard say?"

"I guess he was upset. He didn't say much."

"Where did this happen?"

"At Blake."

"At Blake? You're kidding!"

David could hear the wail of a siren, a warning inside his head. This news changed everything. Blake was on their Native ground and any crime committed on reservation land was tribal business to be enforced by its people.

"Does Richard or Lola know this happened at Blake?"

"I don't know."

David leaned forward. "Tell Maria and Victor as soon as possible that they should never tell Richard or Lola this happened at Blake."

Why not tell Uncle Richard?"

"Because your Uncle Richard might make big trouble for this kid and for himself. I know Richard. He may seem like a quiet man to you, one who goes to work every day and minds his own business...but I know a different Richard."

Ramone told his father that Stark had been at Blake before and after Maria's date with Alberto, and that Stark had gone to Ocho Canyon to try Purple 8 because he was writing a book about it. Then Stark explained that after he tried the formula he lost all interest in writing a novel about someone else's family.

"That happened to me, too, when I was selling used cars in El Centro. I took the formula and I had to quit selling cars. It didn't feel right to me."

"Is there anything that can be done about this Alberto?" Ramone asked his father.

"Well, I'm going to help Pete get caught up and I'm gonna trace on it and see what comes up. I suggest you guys do the same. And we'll see what we can come up with. I'll say this much...this guy with Maria...he's young?"

Ramone and Stark nodded yes.

"The guy's scared by this news. He could change his tune and step up to be in the child's life some day."

Ramone understood where his father was coming from, since he had not come into their lives or offered to help his mother until recently.

204

"I'll be right back," David said.

They both traced their 8s for ten minutes, until David returned and asked them what they felt would make Maria's situation better.

"Maybe Maria should take the formula while she's pregnant. I think she'd feel better."

"Monica and Robert would know if that would be safe for her and her baby," David replied. "What are you prepared to do to help her?"

"I would be willing to go to Omaha."

"That's good. How about you, Stark? What do you feel about this?"

"I would go with Ramone."

"Why would you do that?" David sounded puzzled.

Stark wished he had done something to stop that jerk from using her. He thought any other guy would be lucky to have a girl like Maria. He said, "I'd tell her what a great person she is and what a great mother she'll be...and that this one mistake could turn out to be the best thing that ever happened to her."

David was impressed, nodding his head yes, while his eyes went from Stark to his son.

"Dad, what do you feel can help Maria?"

"I remember how your mother began her remarkable recovery when you and Victor made your video. She began to believe that the people she loved really wanted to help her. And she got to see herself transforming.

"You're right," Ramone said. "She changed right before our eyes. Like magic."

"That's what a baby does to a woman...it changes her."

Stark smiled. "Yeah, it makes her look fat...and kinda ripe."

Ramone bristled. "It's not your place to make

remarks about Maria!"

David interrupted them. "Speaking of places, Ramone, I didn't lose my place in the family just because I divorced your mother. I gave Ocho Canyon to Robert because I thought that Purple 8 could never be marketed to anyone but Native people. He's always been an experimenter. He believed in Purple 8 and in his ability to work out any problems with it. So Ocho Canyon became his place, and mine was to screw up my life. We don't want that to happen to Maria."

"Not a chance, with me around," Ramone declared.

"The way I see it, if you can help Maria through this period in her life, then Purple 8 has done good things for all of us. She's going to need your help Ramone, because Richard will be a silent brooder, until the baby comes. Then he will be Grandpa Richard and love the baby like any of his children."

"I could take a couple of weeks off work around mid-December and be with her over the holidays. Victor could film her progress. Like you said, it really did help Mom when the family got involved." Ramone fell silent, deep in thought.

Stark stopped himself from jumping in and telling them that he wanted to go to Omaha and help rescue her. Sitting in the dark bar in Phoenix, he realized that he had always wanted to be the proud son of the man who rescued the miners trapped in shaft number 99. But his father never let him see that hero, only the one-armed bitter man. But, now, he could become the man who rescued Maria, a girl he could never have if not for this 'accident.' If he had stopped them at Blake, he would not have had this chance. Responsibility warred with hope.

"You're right Dad," Ramone said. "I have to help Maria, if I can. Purple 8 is Uncle Robert's dream. Back when I was mad at the world Maria dreamt of going to college and becoming an actress. It was her genuine goodness that led me to Purple 8. I wanted to be happy like she was. If I keep thinking about the harvest and that I will someday live at Ocho Canyon, I will only be living off the good work Uncle Robert has done already, like a parasite. I have to go back to Omaha."

"I'm happy you feel that way Ramone. I had no real dreams when I was young. You'll pick up another dream, and it'll be all yours, not some family legacy you've inherited."

"I hope you're right," Ramone replied.

David smiled. "Me, too. I'm planning on making some changes in my own life, soon. Starting with a new job; this one pays the bills, but it's depressing being around drunks day after day."

"Do you trace while you work?" Stark asked.

"All the time," David said. "Well, I better get back to work. You boys have a lot to keep off your minds," he smiled.

If Not Now...When?

Stark decided to leave Phoenix in mid-December when Ramone planned to go to Omaha. He worked with Ramone until the 12th, then took a couple of days to empty his apartment. Ramone talked him into staying longer so they could drive their vehicles together to Omaha. Stark didn't need much coercing, only the thought of seeing Maria, who was now four months along and determined to raise her baby as a single parent.

Gina called Maria often and helped her keep her spirits up. Maria told Gina that she was an inspiration to her, because she had overcome her problems and healed her own life.

Ramone felt totally free to leave his mother in Arizona, because she was now happily working as a travel agent at an agency just a few blocks from her apartment. Gina told her son that she looked forward to traveling to the exotic places she'd only dreamed of seeing. She was at work when Ramone and Stark hit the road out of Phoenix.

In Wichita, Kansas, they stopped at a Cracker Barrel for a late dinner. There, they decided to drive straight through to Omaha. During their meal, Stark finally told Ramone about the writing he buried at Nine Palms under the Purple 8 stain.

"I wrote about Maria and the anger I felt toward that worthless bum, Alberto. I kept my feelings about her to myself and wanted to leave them in a safe place. I figured I didn't have a chance in hell of telling her myself. I envied that rich boy with the REDVET. I think about her all the time. I realize that she probably doesn't share the same feelings for me. What do you think?"

"I hear ya. But Maria needs security in her life. I don't see you providing that now. I mean, look Stark, you told me you have about a grand to your name. It takes security to win a girl. Economy is everything."

"I know, Mone. And I know I'm just a slug with no college working the phones, but if I had a chance with Maria, I know it would spark me to make good money doing something."

"Like what?"

"I don't know. I'm confused about that. But I know I would work my tail off for her and her baby. I'm sure of that."

"Well, you have to let her know, and see how she feels about you. But I'm sure that, if you told her now, you would only confuse her."

"Yeah."

They arrived in Omaha too late to announce their presence to anyone. Three in the morning wasn't the best time for a visit. Temperature hovering at 24 degrees above zero threatened to freeze their desert blood. Still, after driving all night they couldn't wait to get out of their cars. They donned winter coats, gloves and hats, and walked around the Carillo's neighborhood.

Drifts of snow glowed a bluish tint under the silver sheen of street lights. The sidewalk was clear and sparkled underfoot like crushed diamonds. Ramone showed his friend the theater that his uncle managed and where Victor now worked part-time as a projectionist.

"Does Maria work there?'

"A few hours on weekends in the box office...at least she was. I used to clean up."

"Free movies, huh?"

"Yeah, it was pretty cool. Especially when we were little."

The streets were vacant of traffic as they stretched their stiff legs after the long drive.

"Mone, do you think Maria would go to a movie with me?"

"She might. Ask her."

"I think she's gonna freak when she sees me here."

"Why are you here, Stark?"

"To see if I have a chance with her, and, whether I do, or not...I want to help her."

"Just tell her you came with me 'cause you're moving back home and you wanted to see her and Victor. It's cool, Stark."

Both were tracing without the other knowing. Stark was more tired than Ramone, because Stark had made the trip into a drama and let his mind run him.

By 5 A.M., and after strong coffee in a convenience store, they were both too wired to sleep. At 6 o'clock, they saw a light on in the Carillo house. Richard hugged his nephew and welcomed them in to his home, telling Ramone it was fine that Stark stayed with them as long as he liked. After Richard went back to getting ready for work, Lola joined them. Over more coffee, she broke the news to them that two days earlier Maria had lost her baby by miscarriage.

When Victor came into the kitchen for breakfast, he was surprised to see Stark with Ramone.

"Stark, what are you doin' here, man?"

"He came to see Maria," Ramone said quietly and laughed. "You don't think he came to see you do ya?"

"How's she doing?" Stark asked.

"You know she lost her baby?" Victor asked.

They nodded yes. Discreetly Victor told them, "She's been depressed. But I think my dad's happy about it."

"How'd it happen?" Ramone asked.

"She got sick at school and Mom and Dad took her to the hospital. She'd already lost the baby. They ran some tests and found out she can't ever have kids."

"The doctor said she would miscarry anytime she got pregnant," Lola added when she sat down with them at the table.

Just then, Maria came into the kitchen wearing a dark brown bathrobe; she looked pale. After hugging Ramone and Stark she sat down with them. Lola poured her some juice and a cup of coffee.

"Sorry about your baby," Ramone said.

"Me too," Stark said softly. "I'm very sorry."

Maria slouched forward, raising her cup of coffee using both hands, as if she had to.

Victor swallowed the last of his toast and left to get dressed for school.

"Maria, Uncle Robert sent me some of his new formula for you, if you want to try it. It could help you heal," Ramone said softly.

She shrugged her shoulders, "I'll be okay," she said.

Stark asked, "Is there anything we can do for you?"

"No thanks, but that's sweet," she sighed.

"You're outta school for awhile?" Stark asked her.

"Yeah, for another week, or so."

"Hey, I'll grab a shower and a nap, then later you can show me around Omaha," Stark said.

"Oh, I don't know...."

"You should get out of the house," Lola said to her daughter. "Take him to Old Town. You always enjoy going there."

Ramone gave Victor a ride. By the time they reached the high school some six blocks away, Ramone had told his brother about Stark's feelings for Maria and about the pages he had buried at Nine Palms the day Maria got pregnant.

Victor said, "The last couple days have been rough on her after losing her baby and finding out she can't ever have another. She's on drugs for depression, Mone. Maria's never needed anything like that, she's always up. I heard my dad tell my mom in Spanish that it's a blessing in disguise, and that she can adopt like they did. I've never seen her so down. Somehow we gotta get her to take Uncle Robert's formula."

"It's easier to take now. She doesn't have to fast. I told her about it. I can't push her."

"Okay."

"Stark's not into writing that book on Purple 8 now. He said he was into it because of Maria, he wanted to impress her."

When the bell rang, Victor said, "See ya after school. Great to have you back for the holidays." Victor smiled and bolted out of Ramone's car.

Stark lay on Ramone's twin bed. He had told Maria he would nap for a couple of hours and then they could go downtown to Old Town. He was mulling over these new images of Maria, so weak and vulnerable and not at all resembling the carefree, confident young woman he met last summer. And yet—she was still so incredibly beautiful to him. To be denied natural motherhood did not seem such a big deal after his terrible youth in Carbonville. It was worse to be born and not wanted by one of your parents. Purple 8 could help her adjust to the situation, he was certain of that.

Maria was also resting on her bed. Her room had become a feminine prison to her now: pink walls with white lace curtains; dozens of stuffed animals; her doll collection; and, a vanity table loaded with colorful perfume bottles. All these things she now thought childish for a girl who had brought death into this world. She had cried more tears since she lost her baby than in her entire life. It reminded her of Gina's crying episodes late at night in Blake, after one of her drinking binges. She wondered how long she would continue beating herself up for making one mistake.

Early in her pregnancy she was clear that she didn't want to know the gender of her baby until it was born. She still didn't know, and now she believed she had been intuitively protecting herself from a lifetime of haunting images.

Always, her place was 'the good girl' who got good grades, who would go to college, and live the kind of rewarding life her parents had worked so hard for. But now, her heart was broken and her body numbed by drugs to the point she felt hollow inside. Now she couldn't cry if she wanted to. Suddenly, she decided to stop taking all medications and try her uncle's formula. Tomorrow she would call Ocho Canyon and find out how long she should be off the antidepressant before taking Purple 8. This alone gave her hope for the future.

By noon, Maria was dressed and ready to leave the house for the first time since leaving the hospital. Lola was happy, until her daughter told her she was not taking anymore pills.

Stark drove Maria to Old Town. Snow began falling in big flakes as they strolled the sidewalk lined with antique shops, gift shops and art galleries. Stark talked louder than usual because Maria wore fuzzy blue earmuffs she kept lifting off her ear whenever he spoke to her. They stopped to look in every window, pointing at things that caught their eyes.

Maria felt good to be out, losing herself in rustic storefronts adorned with country Christmas decorations and wonderful, exotic gifts. In one gallery window a framed acrylic oil painting of a desert landscape with snowcapped mountains captivated her.

"Isn't it beautiful?" she asked, pointing it out to Stark.

Upon seeing the $450.00 price tag, he commented, "Yes...and expensive."

"It looks like someplace in New Mexico or Arizona, doesn't it?"

"Yes, or Mexico."

"Victor could've done something like this."

"He showed me some of his drawings. He is good."

"Now I know why it seems familiar. It reminds me of your story...the one I read in your car."

He wanted to talk to her about a thousand things, anything but the ordeal she'd just been through. And yet, that day at Blake, he yearned to tell her now that he could have stopped the rape because he saw them there. He wanted her to know the words he had written about her that day, and how he left them at Nine Palms under the earth. And she was right: the painting could've been in his story. But now, her interest in his book made him feel like writing again, knowing she would read it.

They went to a restaurant to have a late lunch and to get out of the snow that was piling up fast. Across from each other at a front window booth, he could see signs of the ordeal she had been through on her face.

"I haven't even talked to Gina since the miscarriage.

214

My mom called her and Monica a couple days ago, right when you guys left Phoenix. So now it's official: everyone knows a bad thing happened to me."

"Why label it a bad thing?"

"What do you mean?"

"Your uncle told me something when we were headed for Flat Rock. He said that the mind labels and judges things good or bad, in order to control the ego's need to keep fear and form alive."

"What are you saying?"

"You had an experience that was judged bad by your mind. And yet one day you may see it as a good thing...like if you adopt a baby...or...if the world blows itself up...things like that. Things happen that give you a new perspective."

"Someday...maybe...if those things happen."

"Yeah, but if not now...when?"

"You're saying I can lose this depression now...if I want to...even though I have all these drugs in my system?"

"You said you stopped taking them today."

"Yeah, I did."

"Well, now you are better, right?"

"Yeah."

"Build on that. When my mind starts thinking about stuff that makes me feel bad...I step back and observe it telling me these things. That's when I do what Ramone and Robert taught me...."

"I know...trace your purple 8," she rolled her eyes.

"It works, Maria! When I trace...my mind is not bothering me with past or future crap. After a while I go to it automatically...and my mind loses its control over me."

"Is that why you and Ramone came here...to convince me to take Purple 8? Well, I already decided I want to try it."

"That's great! But that's not the only reason." He hesitated.

She waited for his other reason, until she smiled and said, "If not now...when?"

"That day you went with Alberto? I drove down Hwy. 8 looking for billboard locations for Ramone, and I saw his red vette parked at Blake."

"Oh my God! Did you tell Ramone?"

"Yeah, but he knows to keep quiet so your dad doesn't find out."

"My dad would be so.... I can't think about it!"

"Then don't!" He smiled. " I had a bad feeling about Alberto...and I never would've barged in on your date, but when I heard you were pregnant...I wish I had. Those are the things that bug you...the things you should've done. Mind stuff. So...I trace...."

"Stark?" She smiled at him.

"What?"

"Teach me how to trace."

The Best Christmas

Maria talked to Monica on the phone for an hour after spending the afternoon with Stark at Old Town. She informed her aunt that she was ready to take the formula and had stopped taking her meds. Monica told her to avoid solid foods and to drink lots of water, along with a vitamin/protein drink she could find at a health food store. After five days she would be ready to take the formula. Then, Monica said, she could fast for three more days to get the best results.

Ramone and Stark took Maria to buy the protein drink. That night, Maria announced to her parents that she was preparing to take Uncle Robert's formula. Richard was not happy about it, but Lola defended their daughter, telling him she was an adult, now, and could make her own choices.

Ramone and Victor were elated to hear that Maria would be the third Carillo to take the formula. Later, Victor told Stark, "There is a force at work that may lead us all to the harvest...somehow...because we all let it go."

Victor was grateful for Maria's change of attitude, telling Stark that ever since he and Ramone had arrived her health had improved dramatically.

Stark asked Victor to drive with him to Old Town. Stark wanted his opinion of the painting that had caught Maria's eye.

"It certainly is rich in color, and the work of a real pro. The frame is worth two hundred at least. I would say the price is about right; but isn't it a bit expensive for my sister? I mean you don't have that much money, Stark, to be spending so much on a gift."

"She really liked it. I want her to have it."

"Are you trying to buy her love?"

"Maybe," he smiled. "She's the only girl I ever wanted to buy something like this for."

"Suit yourself. I hope you're not disappointed."

"What are you saying Victor?"

"Look how her last long distance relationship turned out."

"That's why she deserves this gift. She's really been through a rough spell."

"Yeah, it is a nice gift. Are you going to wrap it?"

"I thought I'd have you leave it by the Christmas tree just like this.

On December 24th, Stark called his mother from a busy truck stop in Missouri and told her he'd be home before she went to bed. After he hung up the phone, he walked around the truck stop's interior, getting good vibes about things as he traced.

He went outside and walked around the parking lot, resisting the urge to write down all the ideas that were coming to him without effort. Instead, he chose to reflect on his last few days in Omaha with the Carillos.

When he left early that morning, Maria was still in her room and beginning her third and final day of fasting after taking Robert's formula. Most of the last few days, Maria had kept to herself in her room. Everyone was concerned for her, yet Ramone and Stark both knew that she was processing past emotional pain. When she did come into the kitchen to get lemon water, or to take her daily protein drink they could all see that she was okay.

A couple of nights earlier, on her first night after taking the formula, they were all watching a movie in the family room with the Christmas tree blinking its colorful lights, when Maria had left halfway into the movie and vanished into her room for the rest of the night.

Stark now remembered the expression on Richard's face when his daughter left the room. It was the worried look of a father who did not altogether trust his brother's formula and its prescribed fasting.

Later, when her husband left the room after the movie to go to bed, Lola said, "When Richard moved us to Omaha, I knew that he wanted to raise the children away from David. When Robert persuaded David to take his formula in prison, Richard did not want his children around Purple 8, or David, if he moved back to El Centro. My husband's place in the Carillo family, as the youngest son, was always the least influenced by the harvest. He was third in line to live at Ocho Canyon. Richard wanted to prove that he didn't need their legacy, that Maria didn't either. Somehow he feels that now she will give Purple 8 all the credit for the good things in her life."

Stark said, "It's all about an unshakable place we all inherit in a family. Richard's place is real for him, just like each of us has a place that follows us wherever we go, and is there no matter what happens to us in our lives. Purple 8 will never remove that place within us, because it's rooted in the very essence of who we are. No formula, fasting or tracing can change the past. It will always be there. But we don't have to let our place run our lives in our minds. That's the miracle of Robert's formula. We learn that thoughts are not what or who we are. It gives us back control. Richard doesn't need Purple 8 to know he's a good father...a good man. That's his place...and a good one."

"That's beautiful!" Lola smiled and hugged Stark. "Just the right words."

"Yeah Stark, you really are a writer!" Ramone grinned at his friend.

Stark chuckled to himself. Then thought about last night, when he had said goodbye to Ramone and Victor in Victor's room, while Maria slept in the next bedroom.

Ramone had said, "Stark, I know that we were all friends before you met Maria. And I hope we stay friends, no matter what. What you said about places really helped me let go of the harvest...in a good way. I know it's there, but I can't let the thought of it run my life."

"Me too," Victor said. "I'll make sure Maria sees your gift by the tree Christmas morning."

"I never told her what happened to me that day she was with Alberto. I got to experience what it was like to care about someone besides myself."

"Why don't you tell her this stuff?" Victor said.

"She doesn't need any guy around her right now."

"What are you going to do back home?" Ramone asked.

"No plans. Something will come to me."

Now, Stark got into his car at the truck stop and continued his drive across Missouri on I-40. He still had no clue what he would do after the holidays. Whenever his mind went to that place, the same place that was there when he left Carbonville for Shiloh, he would trace his purple 8, and the unknown future would not drain him of energy. Just learning to trace when his busy mind was running nonstop had changed him. He smiled as he drove and traced, this time not bothered by a thousand uncertainties, as he had been when he left home for the first time.

On Christmas morning, Maria was shocked to see the painting leaning against packages near the tree. She sat on the floor in front of it, staring at it without touching it. She asked herself why Stark would spend so much on her. She remembered their drive through the dust storm, their animated conversations about his book, the date shakes, and his mismatched eyes.

To her, his father's blue eye was the one she noticed first when she looked at him. When they had stopped the second time for a date shake in the Arizona desert, his blue eye looked wounded compared to his brown eye.

As she held her gaze on his gift, she admitted to herself that she had known that he liked her then. Now, after her miscarriage, she knew what it was like to feel a one-sided love.

She was aware that tracing was moving her further away from her dream to be an actress; and, she was now able to say goodbye forever to a girl's fantasy of being rescued by her knight in shining armor, a sobering lesson to learn.

Because of Stark, she could now see that her happy world had never been real; that sort of wishful thinking had died with her baby. That had been her place, a place inspired by movies, hundred of movies at The Jupiter, and inspired by doting parents who never let her hear of the struggles they endured for her sake.

At Blake, only Gina and Ramone had been real. They were free to be mad at God, or David, or each other. Yes, she and her brother had been spared the drama by living at the other end of Blake, that other place in Blake where things were kept quiet, purposely hushed away, in order to show the children that there was still a part of their world far removed from the chaos Uncle David had brought to the family.

But now she traced. That was the greatest gift of all to her. Stark had shown her how to trace in the Old Town restaurant on the day she noticed this painting in the window. She smiled at the painting and knew that this was her best Christmas.

David's Place

Ramone and Victor called David at his apartment on Christmas Day to wish him a merry Christmas. His sons told him that Maria had lost her baby. He was glad to hear that his niece had taken Robert's formula and that her spirits had improved.

When David hung up the phone after talking to the boys, he knew what he had to do. He called his boss at the bar and told him there was a family emergency and that he needed a few days off.

David rented a car and drove to Yuma in search of Alberto Salazar. Alberto was in big trouble, because now there was no Carillo baby to be hurt by the justice David had been born to meet out. As the eldest son, David's place was to avenge any crime against a family member. Richard and Robert, bound by family tradition, would have agreed that it was David's place to find the offender and punish him. According to Carillo tradition, if David ignored his duty to the family—none of his sons could inherit Ocho Canyon. By that same tradition, all of the brothers knew that if David failed to get justice, then Robert, and then Richard were in line for the job.

By the time David reached Yuma he had a plan. It had to work perfectly in order for him to stay out of prison. First he had to find the creep named Alberto who had raped his niece. He wasn't listed in the Yuma phone book.

David drove around to several Yuma credit unions, since Victor had said that Alberto worked at one, but hadn't known which. No REDVET. Without sleep he scoured street after street, until he decided to nap in the rented car at a truck stop east of Yuma on I-8. There would be no motel receipts or credit cards used while on this mission.

The next morning he filled his tank with gas and ate a big breakfast in the truck stop café. Again, he scoured the small city, beginning in the business district, then out into the surrounding neighborhoods. At the end of another day of fruitless searching, he got lucky. He had parked his car on a side street to take stock of the situation. To relieve his frustration, he began to trace his figure-8. Then it came to him. The vette had to be serviced at the local Chevy agency. Someone there could give him Alberto's address. It took him five minutes, and some charm to get what he needed from the girl working at the service bay front counter.

He drove to the upper class neighborhood, but did not see Alberto's car parked anywhere near the house. So, David waited a block away around the corner, knowing his quarry had to pass by him in order to get home.

Finally, after 5 P.M., the vette sped down the street. A young Latino was driving. He parked the vette in the driveway beside the house.

By 8, David was hungry and resigned to staying up all night so he could follow Alberto when he left for work in the morning. But around 9 he saw the vette backing out of the drive.

He followed REDVET to a strip mall, where the young man went into a video store. David began to trace. He had no weapon and hadn't planned how he would get Alberto into his car.

When Alberto came out of the video store, David

followed him again, this time to a house on the outskirts of town.

Again he waited, tracing for over two hours, until a young Latino woman came out of the house alone, got into Alberto's vette and drove away. David's mind was clear now. Five minutes later, David went up to the front door and knocked. Alberto opened the door. David could smell marijuana.

"Are you Alberto Salazar?"

"Yes," he answered, confused and stoned.

"Your girlfriend had an accident in your car a couple minutes ago and she asked me if I'd tell you and give you a ride to her. She's pretty upset."

"Is she okay?"

"Yeah, but she's waiting for the police to get there. Oh, and she said she can't find your registration or insurance card."

"They're in the glove box."

"Look man...I'm just the messenger."

"Okay, just a minute."

David got behind the wheel just as Alberto hurried out of the house and climbed onto the front passenger seat of the rental car.

When David drove onto I-8 going west, Alberto asked him where he was going.

"To Blake."

"Blake? Where's that?"

"About sixteen miles west of El Centro."

"Hey man, what is this?"

He could see that Alberto was terrified.

"You remember Blake don't ya?"

"I don't know a Blake. Who are you?"

"I'm a federal narcotics agent. You were seen coming out of Blake, where we found a hundred pounds of

Mexican weed stashed inside a sofa."

"This is crazy, man. I don't sell pot. I smoke a little for recreation, but I'm no dealer. My old man is vice president of 1st Yuma Credit Union. I'm sure his attorney will want to hear about this."

"Well, we'll see. You just sit there quietly, or we can stop and I'll cuff ya and put ya in a cage. Or, I'll have ya back home in a couple of hours. You'll either be cleared, or you can call your rich daddy to bail you out."

For ten minutes David traced his purple 8 to stop his busy mind. At the Imperial Sand Dunes, David pulled off at the rest area that was located between 8-East and 8-West. While he had been tracing he had seen many things, one of which was the fact that this frightened kid reminded him of his own sons too much to carry out the dictates of some antiquated family tradition. He parked the car at the rest area and turned off the engine.

"Look Alberto...I'm not a federal agent. I'm Maria Carillo's uncle. And I intended to kill you for raping my niece."

"Rape? I didn't rape her!"

"Did she tell you to stop?"

David could see that the young man was telling the truth when he said, "Honestly, I don't know. I'd been smoking weed. We both had."

"Did you know she miscarried the baby?" David asked.

Alberto's nod said yes. "Maria called me and told me she lost the baby."

"You were both stupid for not having protection." Another positive nod and David continued. "I got a Mexican girl pregnant when I was married. I was stupid. I lost two sons for most of their lives. In that way you're lucky. You won't have to live your life knowing deep down in your heart that you brought a child into this world that you didn't want. Can you see that Alberto? I mean really see what I'm telling you here?"

"Yeah. I think you're telling me that you've made some mistakes...and you've learned from them. Do you think I should give Maria some money? I mean...would that help her?"

"I don't think she needs money. I think a phone call telling her how sorry you are for what happened would help. Most of all, it'll do you some good to complete things between you."

"Yeah," Alberto agreed with his head bowed.

"I changed my mind about killing you...unless you ever mention any of this to anybody."

"Oh, I won't, sir."

Alberto opened the passenger door and scrambled out. Before he could mention the letter he intended to write Maria, his captor drove off onto I-8 continuing west.

David was certain that Purple 8 had saved Alberto's life. He drove to Blake and let himself in with the key kept above the door. He slept on the sofa at the scene of the crime.

In the morning he dragged the sofa to the rental car and hauled it to a landfill a few miles away.

David called Robert from a pay phone to let him know he was in town. The Ochos met him at an El Centro pancake house for breakfast. He told them about kidnapping Alberto in Yuma and his plan to kill the bastard for what he had done to Maria at Blake.

"But I couldn't do it. I traced and it just wasn't an option to harm him. So I let him go and suggested he apologize to Maria. I spent the night at Blake and hauled that couch to the dump. So much for the violent side of the Carillo tradition." David shrugged.

Robert wasn't displeased with his brother's failure to live up to family expectations. "You may not have killed Alberto, but you did kill the Carillo legacy. And good riddance, I say!"

"Yes, good riddance," Monica agreed. "Ramone must know that this legacy thing can't be legally enforced today. It's not fair to him, if he thinks he's going to move into our house just because he gets married."

Robert told his brother, "You kept the legacy story alive when you wanted to impress Gina. Ramone, Victor and Maria can share equally in the harvest if they want to help market it, but Ramone doesn't just take over. Our father was wrong to use the old traditions to manipulate you; he ended up driving you away from home. Any member of our family who wants to live at Ocho Canyon is welcome. There is enough space for everybody."

Monica grinned at David. "So, when are you moving back to El Centro?" she asked. He just grinned back and gave her a wink.

"You know," David said, "Gina and I should tell the world about Purple 8. We have seen it work miracles in our lives. Just the fact that we are friends again says a lot about Purple 8."

"All of us seem to be thinking about how to market Purple 8," Robert said.

"Ramone and his friend told me that they didn't think the public would ever be ready for a product like Purple 8, that too many idiots out there would try to sue us."

"Yes, that may be true. We'd still be happy if only people on the reservation and our family benefit from the formula," Robert said.

"So Ramone's friend, Stark, he's not going to write his book?" Monica asked David.

"I guess, after his session here he lost interest. He told me he had a thing for Maria and wasn't really serious about writing that kind of story. He was more interested in Maria; when she went out with Alberto..."

"He's young. He'll do what he wants," Robert replied. "But it bothers me that Ramone has lost interest in the harvest."

David spent the night at Ocho Canyon and tried his brother's improved formula without fasting. The three of them spent hours on the back patio talking about the family and their plans for the future. David was on top of everything, as far as knowing what he wanted to do with Purple 8. He surprised the Ochos, when he told them he'd been thinking about the harvest for a long time, even before going to prison.

He said, "I started really thinking about it in Mexico, where I had plenty of time to reflect on it. Ramone's idea to sell Purple 8 to truckers is perfect, now that there is no fasting involved. And Blake is the perfect location to sell it to them. When I was in prison I met an inmate who sold cigarettes to truckers on reservation land by calling them on a CB radio. He did great until the law found out that the smokes were stolen. A lot of ex-cons are truck drivers, and there's no bigger market in need of Purple 8 than men and women just out of prison. Now that I'm here, I'd like to put a couple of well-placed billboards on I-8 and talk to truckers on CB from Blake. This has to be a word-of-mouth thing that grows slowly. I think your formula is needed by the world, brother. It helped me rise above a place I was given long ago. Folks like me ought to have the same chance."

The Harvest

By February 2008, for three months, every morning Robert had made a trek to look behind the canyon walls to see if the harvest had come. He had never seen a mass harvest; he'd only heard legends that he would know it when it came. Yet Robert worried that extremely cold nights during December might have threatened the long-awaited cycle of the blue cactus.

Once again, he hiked from the house to the edge of the canyon wall that obscured the desert floor. His supply of juice had run low because David's plan to market Purple 8 to truckers by CB radio was working like gangbusters. Truckers stopped in an endless yet smooth convoy that filled the open desert parking lot around Blake with big-rigs.

Last fall, Victor and Ramone had moved into Blake with David to help market the formula that had worked miracles in their lives. Victor had completed two years of college at ASU, taking courses in marketing, digital film, and communications. He and Ramone had lived together those last few years in the same apartment in Mesa. Ramone had continued to work for John at Tempe Sign Company and had purchased their billboard graphics and posters at cost. Ramone had picked out three billboard locations: two in Arizona on I-8-West between Casa Grande and Yuma, and one located on the eastern border of the reservation at the Blake exit.

Now, Robert's eyes beheld the harvest. It had come in an explosion of purple he had never seen before. Thousands of the cacti had formed a carpet of deep purple on the canyon floor, ready to supply the family with enough juice to last for a generation, or more. He stood a hundred yards away, staring in wondrous awe, knowing he was the only person on earth to see this.

Maria rode toward El Centro in Gina's white convertible. The top was up because the desert was chilly this time of year. Maria had spent a couple of days relaxing by the pool at Gina's place in Scottsdale. Her travel agent aunt had gotten her a great deal on a flight from Omaha, where she still lived with her parents after graduating with a business degree in marketing from the University of Nebraska in Omaha in just three years.

As the pair neared the exit to I-8 from I-10, Gina told Maria that she had no idea how things were going at Blake.

"Ramone said that we would see when we got there."

Maria smiled at Gina. Her aunt had never looked better. All signs of her paralysis were gone; she moved without stiffness in her lower body. She seemed very happy with her work, and now she was going back to El Centro for a family meeting at Ocho Canyon, where she would see David again. Maria wondered if that had anything to do with her aunt's gaiety.

Maria had been persuaded to return to Blake only because David discreetly told her that the whole place had been transformed. There would be no reminders of Alberto. Both women had been offered a place in the harvest along with Richard and Lola, who had been invited to the meeting, but declined politely. Richard had told his brothers that his

231

place was in Omaha. He wanted no part in the harvest, even though he and Lola believed that the formula had helped the rest of the family, especially Maria.

Over the last few years, all of Maria's energy had gone into school. After the incident with Alberto, she stayed away from dating. Tracing had helped her tremendously, she told Gina. Not once could she remember sitting home and feeling sorry about her lack of a social life.

"Same here," Gina had laughed.

Near the Gila Bend exit, Gina drove past the first Purple 8 billboard with its white background and bold purple print: PURPLE 8. Below that, also in purple letters: Natural Energy for Truckers. And below that: Take the Blake Exit/26 miles west of El Centro.

"It's beautiful," Maria said.

"It catches your attention and is easy to read. I wanted to read it!" Gina exclaimed.

"Me too," Maria smiled, then traced as she watched the Arizona desert flash by her window.

Maria was returning home for the first time since that summer with the boys at Ocho Canyon. The drive brought to mind the letter Alberto had sent her before she started college. He seemed sincere when he wrote that he was sorry about the loss of the baby. Hearing from Alberto out of the blue really had helped her healing process. Because of his letter, she was able to move past her anger at herself for her poor judgment about Alberto. She took responsibility for the choices she made that had gotten her in trouble. Then she put it behind her.

Maria asked Gina to stop at the same spot where she and Stark drank date shakes. They ordered two shakes to go. At the counter, Maria was shocked to see a stack of novels titled *Purple 8* by the cash register. She handed Gina a copy of the book. The cover said: A novel by W. E. Stark.

They each bought a copy and sat down at a booth to begin reading, nearly ignoring their date shakes.

The first chapter was about a young writer in Carbonville who wrote about his youth. Maria read out loud a passage about the writer's mother:

> *How could I greet the new day with a smile in my heart when her pathetic life was all over me. It was there in every shirt on my back that she ironed; it was there in the strong smell of lye she used to clean my father's clothes; and, it was there in my own reflection, for I resembled her far more than my father. There are places in a family we inherit that stay with us for a lifetime, and most of us will hold onto these invisible places as if they define who we are. My parents gave me my place, as the son of a sad mother and an alcoholic father. What else could they do? Sometimes only an outsider, a stranger, can see the place we are given. Even more rare is someone who was assigned an awful place when young...yet manages to escape, to find love in an American family holding its place until the big harvest comes.*

"It's about our family," Maria told Gina. "It's not a novel, it's more like an autobiography."

"I know."

They went back to the register where they bought the books.

"Where did these books come from?" Maria asked the cashier.

"The writer came in a few days ago and we bought them from him." She laughed, "He was a pretty persuasive salesman."

Outside, Maria said, "Stark might be at Blake with David and the boys." For the first time she acknowledged that she had feelings for Ramone's friend.

Maria read to Gina on their drive west. The first chapter in *Purple 8* was about Stark's life in Carbonville as the son of a local hero and a neglected mother. Later in the book, when the fictional Stark left Shiloh, Maria felt she was being allowed to see the author's private thoughts, reading how the character he had created had concentrated on emanating gratitude, which he said would eliminate unnecessary fear and worry, and allow him to be open to good things coming into his life.

"Listen to this," Maria said, and read a few lines.

> *I drove west, following the sun, realizing the gratitude I was feeling came from positive words, from affirmations that I forced my mind to repeat ten thousands times after I left Shiloh, like a broken record. Silence. That had to be the answer, a thing that my mind abhors. I want to find a place where my mind can rest.*

"It's well written," Gina remarked.

"I can't get over the fact that it's all about us and Purple 8," Maria said.

"You're the love interest in the story. You know that, don't you?" Gina asked her niece.

Maria knew it was true. Stark had written what she enjoyed reading, a story about a man who declared his love and risked everything to prove his love was true.

Maria read to Gina all the way to El Centro, where they stopped at a gas station so they could read the last thirty pages of the book. Maria said, "I was wrong. It's not really an autobiography."

"No," Gina agreed, "only the first part of the plot. The rest is pure fiction."

"Thank God!" Maria declared.

Then, as Gina drove down I-8, anticipating the last billboard mentioned in Stark's novel, she said, "Stark's written a beautiful mystery that really held my attention throughout. And it's obvious that it was written for truck drivers; look how he describes going to work at that truck stop in Carbonville, and befriending those two truckers. You know, it's just as obvious that Stark is in love with you."

"No way! He just used me as a character in his story. He had to have someone as a love interest."

They were slowing down in the right lane of I-8 because of heavy truck traffic, as if they were approaching a weigh station. Maria pointed to the right and told Gina to look. There was the last billboard, printed in bold purple letters, exactly like the one that Stark had written about in his book: 'FREE PURPLE 8 at BLAKE EXIT.'

"Look at all the trucks!" Gina exclaimed.

She drove sandwiched between two semis, following the one in front as it made its wide turn onto the road that ran along the open desert on reservation land surrounding Blake. The building's exterior had been painted purple with white doors. There were semi trucks parked in orderly rows all round their old home.

Then Gina got it. "Government regulations prohibit Purple 8 from being sold off the reservation. Free Purple 8 is legal," she said. "Ingenious," Gina muttered as she parked in back of Blake near vehicles that were familiar to them.

As the women walked to the entrance, they estimated that there were at least a hundred semi trucks parked around Blake. Truckers milled in little groups in front of the low building.

Inside Blake, Monica was pouring ginger tea and serving it to truckers waiting in line in the front room to buy a signed copy of *Purple 8* and to get a free sample of the formula. Victor and Ramone were helping Monica, serving the tea throughout Blake. Ramone spotted his mother and gave her a broad wink and a broader smile.

Maria saw Stark seated at a table at the back of the room; he was signing his book for each trucker who paid a $20.00 donation, dropping the money into a five-gallon bucket beside the author.

Five feet away, at another table, Robert handed out free samples of his formula, two purple capsules in paper medicine cups. With each cup he offered three simple words, "Trace and enjoy."

During a break, Ramone and Victor told Maria and Gina that it had been Stark's idea to give away the formula with each book. "Distributing Purple 8 is legal as long as the formula is not sold to the public," Ramone explained.

"I had no idea you would be doing this amount of business," Gina commented. "This is a lot to take in."

"It is," Victor said, "Uncle Robert has agreed to continue publishing Stark's book and to split the donations four ways: Stark gets one share; Monica and Robert get one share; Ramone and you and David split a share; and Maria, Mom and Dad, and I split a share."

Victor grinned when Gina frowned in puzzlement. "That's a lot of us getting money from Purple 8," she said.

"There's gonna be a lot to share," Ramone replied.

Victor led the new arrivals into another room. There they saw two dozen truckers seated on folding chairs, watching Victor's documentary on DVD. Near the end of the film, Victor had added footage of Robert explaining the legal situation regarding selling the formula, and that for a twenty-dollar donation clients would get a copy of *Purple 8* and free capsules. He said, "And feel free to take two capsules of Purple 8, the formula. The more you trace...the better the results."

Gina was truly impressed that most of the truckers filed out of the room after viewing the documentary and got in line for Stark's book and the formula.

Next, Ramone led his mother by her hand, with Maria following them, to the other end of Blake. In Gina's old room, David was seated behind a desk, wearing a headset and talking to truckers on a CB radio, urging them to take the Blake exit.

David removed his headset and gave the girls big hugs. "You both look great," he said. Then David began filling them in on the business. "See, Stark's book told us how to market it to the truckers. Stark really did work at a truck stop in Carbonville. He wrote most of the book there. Anyway, Stark did some test marketing by telling truckers about Robert's formula and asking them questions about their health. He told them if Robert thought the formula could help their health problems, he would let them know by posting the information on the bulletin board. You can guess the rest."

Gina said, "Well, I can see that it's a success."

"Stark self-published the book in Carbonville, five thousand copies. Then, when Robert told him the harvest was near, he started giving the book away to lots of truckers, telling them to read it and pass it on to another trucker. Stark had been giving away copies for weeks, when Robert and Monica noticed all these headlights driving around Blake at night. Semi trucks! Robert called me and told me truckers were driving by Blake because of Stark's book. So, I quit my job the next day and moved in here. I've got a bed in Ramone's old room. Well, then I read the book and we painted Blake purple, just like it was in the book. I even use the phone script from the book while I talk to truckers all day."

"You do this all day?" Gina asked.

"From six to six. Ramone and I take turns."

"Three hours on and three off," Ramone added. "We mix it up. Like he did six to nine this morning and I did six hours straight...and he'll do three to six."

"So Stark gives away his book?" Maria asked.

"All day long." Ramone smiled. "The average donation is thirty bucks. Quite a few of the truckers donate forty bucks, because they want a second copy for someone they know."

"And they get a couple extra Purple 8 pills...just like in the book," Gina stated.

"Another ten thousand copies of the book'll be delivered here next week," David informed them. "There is very little overhead and we're movin' about 200 books a day...seven days a week." David grinned.

"It's working!" Gina laughed.

"No way could we sell the book, or the formula, but we can give them away all day!" David chuckled.

Ramone said, "The truckers love the idea, they'd rather give and get something for it, than buy after being sold."

"Stark says the same thing." David smiled.

Two Reasons It Worked

A little after six that evening, the last trucker left Blake with his signed copy of *Purple 8* and two Purple 8 capsules.

Stark had filled out since Maria last saw him. When he stood up from behind the table, his muscular body impressed her. He looked as if he'd put on fifteen pounds, all of it honed muscle. They embraced and she laughed when she had to catch her breath after he'd squeezed it out of her.

"We could use your help," Stark told the two women.

Maria looked at Gina, knowing that the formula had changed both their lives for the better.

"What would we do here?" Gina asked.

Monica came over and picked up the five-gallon bucket full of cash and personal checks. "Can you count? We need a bookkeeper. There are plenty of other things to do, too. We try to stay on top of it...but it gets tougher every day."

"I don't want to live at Blake," Maria declared.

"No, no, you would both live at Ocho Canyon," Monica said.

"Just try it for a couple weeks, Mom," Ramone pleaded.

"I've got my job at the travel agency, Ramone. I love

my job. I'm going to Europe next month. Free round-trip flights. I'd like to help you, but only this weekend, till I go back Sunday night."

Ramone nodded, indicating he understood.

That's when it dawned on Gina that she now felt the same as David had felt when he was young. She didn't want to be involved here, or live here, because the life she wanted, one she had constructed on her own terms, was somewhere else.

Ramone and Victor turned toward Maria.

"I can stay for awhile. I'm not working in Omaha. I know some basic bookkeeping, but I'm no CPA."

The boys embraced Maria.

That night the eight of them gathered for dinner at Ocho Canyon. The talk at the table was nonstop and full of energy. Gina was happy to see Ramone so excited about the business coming to Blake every day. The fact that she would receive a share in the venture bothered her, because she didn't choose to live there and contribute. When she told the others how she felt about it, Monica assured her, "Your role in the documentary is helping us. Richard and Lola are also getting a share, don't forget."

Stark entered the conversation, "When I first came here, I had less than five hundred copies of my book left, I gave so many away at the Carbonville truck stop. The impact of your recovery on those truckers was the thing that made it easy for me to sell books from Carbonville to California. Word got out and truckers were asking for the book at truck stops. See, Gina, you had an important place in the story, like everyone else in the Carillo family. By the time I got here, our marketing technique was working better than I had ever imagined."

"That's great! And I'm happy for you all," Gina

replied. "But I don't think I've done anything, really. My payment for appearing in the documentary is the good health I have now."

"Gina, that's very unselfish of you. I admire you for your position," Robert said, "But we all disagree."

"All of you?" Gina asked. "What do you mean?"

"Gina, you see that bowl over there?" Stark pointed to the brown clay bowl on the table in the living room into which the Ochos put their mail. "When we started this business, Monica, Robert, David and I agreed that each of us would write down the names of everyone who should get a share of the harvest. We each put a list of names in that bowl. When Victor and Ramone arrived, they each placed a list of names into the bowl. Each one of us had agreed that all ten people should get a share. It was unanimous."

"I'm in the book, too," Maria said, "but I don't see how I contributed."

"Tomorrow I'll show you your contribution." Stark smiled.

Gina and Maria were amazed when, at 5 A.M. the next morning, a fleet of semis were parked in neat rows all around Blake. The idling trucks were a symphony of raw power, all there because word had spread that overnight parking was encouraged, reinforced by the friendly sign beside the Blake front entrance: FREE OVERNIGHT PARKING / OPEN 6 A.M. to 6 P.M.

Monica cooked a big breakfast at Blake. That's how Maria found out that Stark had been sleeping on a mattress on the floor in Victor's old room, surrounded by cases filled with copies of his book.

After breakfast Maria and Gina got to hear David do his thing on the CB radio. He was having a lot of fun talking to truckers, luring them in with his high energy animation, "Purple 8 will wake you up! Say goodbye to the blahs and hello to the energy buzz of your life...and naturally."

Over the radio one trucker remarked, "But I don't read books...."

"For twenty bucks, you'll read this one," David laughed. Then he told the guy he could watch a documentary on the formula, and then make up his mind. "I'm no arm-twisting used car salesman." He looked over his shoulder and grinned at his ex-wife.

Meanwhile Robert, Stark, Victor and Ramone stood together outside Blake's front door watching the 18-wheelers pouring in from I-8 and lining up in perfect rows of idling steel.

"This is beautiful," Robert said.

They all nodded in agreement, each one knowing how lucky he was to be there.

Robert believed that David and Gina were the luckiest of them, because they had taken the longest and most difficult routes, by far. David had told him that he savored this place where his sons were both working with him, and reaping the harvest that once he had turned away from. David confessed that he had always wanted his sons to have this opportunity.

Robert smiled to himself, recalling that Stark had insisted on one condition before agreeing that all the profits be divided into shares. He had demanded that the family legacy be dropped forever. "No more of this nonsense!" Stark had told Robert, adding, "You and Monica have made the blue cactus a valuable product by consistent labor mixed with love. You and Monica should live here as long as you want, and leave it to someone who will care for it."

Robert had replied that the men of the family had to agree. When Ramone and Victor, Richard and David all agreed with Stark's condition, it marked the end of the Carillo legacy. In its place, a new legacy had begun: a family united, working together, each in his own way, for the benefit of all.

Now, Ramone and Victor walked out to greet some of the truckers climbing out of their cabs and headed for Blake.

Stark stood in the open door and gazed at Nine Palms in the distance. Last night he had told Maria that he wanted to take her there to dig up his writing. He had suggested that they could walk to Nine Palms after work when the sun was going down.

Maria had seemed intrigued. "In your book, those words proved that the writer who left them there loved Marie. What will I learn?" she asked.

Another Kind of Place

The sun had dipped below the mountains by the time Maria finished reading the words Stark had buried at Nine Palms. Even though she had read similar words in his book, she read them this time as if they were meant just for her.

They didn't discuss the pages she'd just read. He watched her return them to their place, then he helped her cover them again with the same earth.

On the slow walk back to Blake, she took his hand in hers and they gazed at each other, both thinking of the journey that brought them together. There was no past, no plans for the future, only two knowing smiles that said now is the only time we'll ever have together.

They watched a silver semi truck rolling away from Blake toward I-8, its diesel engine whining and fading. Stark said, "The Carillo legacy is no more. Everyone is free to marry and live wherever they want."

"Why is that so important to you?" she wanted to know.

"Well," he asked, "if you got married and decided to adopt children, would you want them to be stuck in a pile of purple crap?"

Maria laughed joyously and leaned into his shoulder. It felt good to laugh and be with the man who had written about her family and the places they overcame in order to help others.

They stopped walking in fading sunlight that turned everything around them golden. They looked to the west where the sun had begun to set, in the direction of Ocho Canyon, a place that would never hold power over any Carillo again. They fell quiet.

Stark was lost in words that Zane Grey had written long ago:

Places were the most vital and compelling things in the world, next to human life. Perhaps they were more important, because they had evolved life and had sustained it through the course of the ages. Whatever happened to people—birth, growth, trouble, defeat or success, love, passion, joy, loss, death—all were vitally affected by the part of the earth in which they took place.

Just like the shaded place behind them, and the purple building up ahead, those parts of the earth used to be the only places Stark could write about, until he met Maria's incredible family, a family that revealed other places that were just as real as those words of Zane Grey buried at Nine Palms.

Now, as they continued their walk toward Blake, Stark was aware that each sort of place had given him his book. In order to break away from the place he had inherited in Carbonville, he'd had to return home and write Purple 8 away from Maria and her family. He had needed to walk down Main Street and stop in all the places his father knew, where he was still the son of the hero of mine shaft 99. But there had been no fire in his blood, as when his father was alive. At the Carbonville Barber Shop, and in his father's favorite tavern, the men his father had worked with and rescued were now also free to see Lefty's son as he truly was.

Lefty had chosen his place—on a barstool in a dark

tavern, indulged by the men he had saved. His was a dark place, numbed with alcohol and old stories.

Stark, too, had chosen his place. This was his place—to be here now with Maria. He wrapped his arm around her slim waist and pulled her close.

"When you are young," he said, "you are given a place that influences who you let into your life. You make mistakes and keep repeating them, until you choose to change. When you make this change, it always involves other people who are close to you, who are confused and injured by your move. This is the necessary pain of growth from loss. My book is about actively choosing your place. I wanted it to be easy for readers to recognize what they had been doing to themselves unconsciously."

Maria smiled up at him. "And truckers like your book because they are alone more than most people. That is their place and your book helps them accept it."

Stark said, "Really, we're all alone, when it comes down to it. We all have to make peace with that place."

THE END

Librarians and readers interested in
Michael Frederick titles and information
on his first book signing tour may
E-mail: mfrederick310@aol.com
or write to: Michael Frederick
PMB 246, 14245 S. 48th Street
Phoenix, AZ 85044